A CURSED NOËL

A Weird Girls Novella

CECY ROBSON

The Carolina Beach Novels
Inseverable
Eternal
Infinite

In Too Far Novels
Salvatore

Death Seeker Novels
Unearthed

APPS
Crazy Maple Studios Chapters Interactive Stories
Crazy Maple Studios Kiss Romance

Hooked – Chat Stories
(Cecy Robson writes as Rosalina San Tiago)

Praise for the Weird Girls series

"One of my favorite books series . . . so much action, so much violence and, oh, the lust radiating off of our heroes . . . I definitely recommend this series for lovers of all things paranormal and awesome." *–USA Today*

"Robson's blend of smart-alecky wit, good old-fashioned romance, and suspenseful episodes of fighting off evil spirits form a paranormal thriller that will make pulses pound." **–Publishers Weekly**

"I would devour anything that Ms. Robson writes. I strongly recommend [the Weird Girls] series to PNR/UF readers and fans of Larissa Ione, Kresley Cole and Gena Showalter. Cecy Robson is pretty up there, IMO." **–Under the Covers Book Blog**

When I started reading the Weird Girls series a few years back, I fell deeply in love with Cecy Robson's sharp, funny dialogue, hilarious characters and brilliant world building. **–Book and Movie Dimension**

"I love this series! It is funny, action filled, and filled with hot para awesomeness." **–Delphina Reads Too Much**

"[Of Flame and Light] Most action-packed/thrilling/unputdownable book of the year [2016] and Best Sequel and Series Ender...Tara Wird –most memorable character of 2016." **–The Reading Cave**

"[With Robson's] edgy, witty and modern style of storytelling, the reader will be drawn deep into this quirky paranormal world . . . Strong pacing, constant action and distinctive, appealing characters—including a gutsy heroine—will no doubt keep you invested." *–RT Book Reviews*

"A healthy dose of humor, a heaping dash of the supernatural, and a pinch of mystery all laced with a heavy dollop of action . . . Robson knows how to combine all the best ingredients to keep her readers hooked and begging for another hit." *–Fresh Fiction*

"...Robson's supernatural tale will leave readers clawing for the next installment." *–Booklist*

"Page after page it's packed with non-stop action, a lot of conflicts and well-developed characters. The Weird Girls is a fast-paced read, one I can guarantee you, you won't be able to put down." **–The Bookaholic Cat**

"I was blown away by the depth of passion, humor, and creativity in this story...If you are a fan of powerful, sarcastic heroines and cross-over urban fantasy / paranormal romance stories, I highly recommend *Of Flame and Light.*" **–Grave Tells Romance**

"Why do I love this series so much? Ms. Robson is a master at blending hilarious humor and scorching romance with her imaginative crazy action and fight scenes." **–Addicted to Happily Ever After**

DEDICATION

To Mair, who always had my back.

CHAPTER ONE

The plane starts its descent toward the small airport outside of my hometown. Clouds skim past the window, unveiling the Colorado mountains as the sun begins to rise.

I ignore the magnificence and beauty, barely registering that snow no longer blankets the treetops and that Spring isn't far away. Hell, I barely notice anything anymore, my full focus on my next kill, and the one after that.

Where will I go next time? The Besakih Temple in Bali? Or maybe a barren countryside in Moldova? I flex my grimy fingers. Will my beast's claws dig deep and tear my opponent apart like the last rogue vampire I encountered? Or will my fangs snap his head clear from his shoulders like that lone wolf who double-crossed me?

Who knows? Who cares? I sure as hell don't. Just point the way and me and my beast will take care of the rest.

"Do you need a ride home, Aric?" Blaze asks.

He does that. Tries to get me to talk, I mean.

"I'm good," I say, but not much more. I'm not trying to be a prick. I just don't say much anymore.

I add a thanks. It's the least I can do. Blaze is good about flying me where I need to be. Sometimes it's just here in the States. Lately it's to a larger airport where I can catch a flight across oceans and continents. Blaze has never complained, and I've given him plenty of reasons.

Just today, I woke him hours before dawn. I needed a ride and, like usual, I'm covered in blood.

Blood is nothing new to me. I wear the lifeline of others like a second skin. The scent, the sticky feeling right before it dries, and how it conforms to my body revitalizes my drive to hunt.

There should be something wrong about it. But I bask in it.

This is the blood of my enemies, and they deserved to die.

We're on the ground and taxiing toward the hanger a few minutes later. I hop out before Blaze cuts the engine, ignoring the crew of *weres* who hurry forward to secure the plane.

They stopped greeting me a long while ago. They *don't* stop bowing their heads, the one thing I wish they would do. As a pureblood *were*, I'm deemed as royalty. It doesn't mean anything. Cut off my head or shoot me in the heart with gold bullets and I'm as good as dead.

Or cast just the right curse and I'll die, just like my dad.

My dad...

My heart clenches. It's been two years and his loss doesn't hurt any less.

"Aric, wait," Martin calls.

My alpha doesn't yell. He doesn't have to. My hearing would pick up his deep baritone from far away. I slow my speed, feeling the power of the command down to my beaten-down boots.

Martin, satisfied that I won't take off in a run like last time, stalks away from the large group gathered by the terminal.

As usual, a crowd of females have gathered in anticipation of my arrival. My kind possesses high metabolisms. It takes a lot to make us cold. Still, their barely-there clothing doesn't seem right considering they're clearing two inches of ice from the tarmac just a few yards away.

One of them, God help me, is waving a sign. "Welcome Home Aric Connor," it reads.

I know my name, thanks.

I try not to roll my eyes when the redhead in front blows me a kiss. She thinks I'm playing hard to get. But games are for kids, and I grew up fast.

The one with the sign shakes it harder, like I didn't notice the fluorescent pink hearts and glitter the first time.

"Aric Connor Groupies." That's what Liam called them. He meant to make me laugh, except laughing no longer comes easy.

Martin reaches me. Like me, he ignores my "fans." "Let's talk," he says.

"Can't," I say. "Gotta get home."

"I wasn't asking," Martin says, his tone clipped.

I reduce my speed, not realizing I'd picked up my pace as I neared the crowd. He motions in the direction of his dark blue Lexus SUV.

"Fine," I mutter, shifting direction.

I throw open the door and slip inside. Some of the drying blood flakes onto his pristine white leather seats. I kill the smirk that starts to form. Martin notices anyway.

He raises his brows. I shrug. He's the one who wanted to talk.

With a gentle hum, the engine comes to life and Martin rolls toward the exit. "I want you to stop hunting," he says.

I huff. He's not talking about elk.

The frown I'm sporting deepens when we reach the gate and I catch sight of Mimi, Liam's batshit-crazy aunt. The behemoth weregrizzlies on guard duty give her ample space. Smart *weres*. Mimi is old, mean, and nuttier than a van full of killer clowns. The last *were* who offended her sprouted fangs on his navel and watched in horror as it chewed off his toes.

She waves an age-spotted hand at me, her gray lips pulling back to show me the remainder of her crooked teeth. I don't exactly smile back. That would just invite more of the crazy and who the hell needs that?

My snub only delights her. Several more wrinkles form around her beady black eyes, her enthusiasm inching the grizzlies further away from her.

What's this crazy hag up to?

Her smile widens and she cackles as if she can hear me. Maybe she can. *Hags* skitter that fine line between merrily insane and unleash-a-plague-upon-the-earth-because-I'm-a-bored-psychotic. Still, the magical punch they pack can wipe out a cyclone swimming with weresharks. It's why my kind both respects and fears them.

Clumps of Mimi's curly gray and white hair slap against her curved spine and tendrils of smoke spill from the hem of her black dress as she levitates toward a walkway. Mimi rarely leaves her cave in the mountains. When she ventures down, it's usually to cause trouble. I'm surprised she's lasted this long without being burned at the stake. At the very least, someone should have stoned her crazy ass.

"Aric, are you listening?" Martin asks.

No. I'm watching Mimi.

Just like she's watching me.

"Aric!"

Martin's voice is the equivalent of a slap upside the head. He was always patient with me, but after putting up with my crap these last few years, that patience is as dead as the last *were* who crossed Mimi.

Instead of cowering, like any prey at Martin's mercy would, I bare my teeth. I don't hide from a fight, ever. "What's your problem?" I snarl. "As a *were*, I have a sworn duty to guard the earth and the unsuspecting human populace from the shrouds of evil."

Martin mutters something that sounds more wolf than human. He dismisses my insolence and turns onto the highway. He thinks I won't attack. He should think again.

"I know what our roles as Guardians of the Earth entail. I don't need reminding, Aric."

"Then why'd you ask?" I grumble. "Every mission I've taken has wiped out the evil overtaking our planet and saved lives. I'm just doing my damn job."

"You're really pushing me with that mouth of yours," Martin growls. He drags his hand down the smooth dark skin of his face, trying to reign in his wolf.

Martin is known for his cool head and reason. I have a funny way of kicking both attributes in the nuts. He needs to back off and understand I want to be left alone. I think back to my mother. *Well, maybe not all alone.*

"Aric, you're the only *were* in history to achieve his *change* before six months of age. You're special...."

Oh, boy, here we go.

"You should be in school, learning and developing your gifts as a future alpha...."

My attention drifts to a stand of oak trees lining the road. Mimi is sitting on one of the lower branches, her tiny feet swinging as she munches on what looks like roasted squirrel on a stick. She grins at me through a rather large bite.

Seriously, what is this old hag up to?

"Aric, your pack and your friends need you. While your advanced strength and agility permit you advantages older and more experienced *weres* don't possess, there's a great deal more to learn. You should be training with your kind, not flying halfway around the world on assignments that should require more than one *were* and a strategy that requires more than simply mauling your prey."

"I work better alone, and mauling is strategy enough for me," I counter.

Martin cuts right and up the mountain. "It's worked so far," he says. "But you've been lucky. These missions aren't ones that should be taken lightly. One mistake, that's all it will take to lose you."

"Maybe." I shrug. "But it's better than sitting on my ass like you."

A roar unlike anything I've ever heard from Martin breaks free of his throat. "*Do not disrespect me. Not as your alpha. Not as your father's best friend. You owe him more than that,"* he growls.

"And as his Beta and Warrior you owed him your life. Not the other way around," I growl in return.

Martin stomps on the brakes. We face off, our chests heaving in and out with how hard our wolves charge to the surface. He wants to fight? Let's go. *I'm not afraid, old man.*

Silence fills the cabin. That, and rage. For several long minutes, that's all there is. I'm so angry, I'm sick from it. The hate I feel toward Martin—the world—*everything* rages through me with enough menace to crush my bones.

My father shouldn't have died. He shouldn't have left my mother a shell of the female she once was. *Damn it. He shouldn't have left me!*

I was only fifteen. I needed him—to be my father, to be my best friend. How could he go down the way he did? Someone so good didn't deserve to die. Not like that.

My fury triggers the memory, the one I fight to push down. But there it is, front and center, making me relive the worst moment of my life.

We were in the kitchen when we felt him pass. Mom was at the stove, cooking ground venison for the shepherd's pie she was making. We missed Dad. She was trying to lift my spirits by making one of my favorite dishes. I was trying to make her smile by sharing something Liam had done. Her head tilted up to laugh, only for her skin to pale and her face to scrunch with agony.

I reached for her, my hand disappearing as a tundra of sorrow blinded me and brought me to my knees. I didn't understand what was happening until every emotion I felt for Dad knocked into me: Love, awe, respect, even fear. And then.... *nothing.*

He was gone. I knew it. I recovered first, demanding answers. Mom just laid there, her blank stare toward the ceiling and barely alive. I snatched her up into my arms, begging her not to leave me.

After years of trying, I was her only child. As cruel as it was, I used it to my advantage, telling her I'd be alone if she left me too.

As mates, she should have died by the rise of the next full moon following my father's passing. But as much as she loved my father, she couldn't leave the one thing they cherished most.

So, she stayed. But only barely.

On a good day, Mom will leave her bed and shower. Maybe cook dinner. Maybe do some laundry. On a bad, she doesn't leave her room. She just lays in bed, staring at the bedside photo of their wedding day. She barely eats enough to sustain her inner beast, and now her hair is falling out in chunks.

"Aric," Martin says. The weight of the guilt he carries materializes in the way he speaks my name. Martin doesn't want me to hunt. He doesn't want me to hurt. He doesn't understand that hunting is how I beat back the pain, and is the only way to placate my beast. I'm trying to hang onto the life I have left, and *weres* like him aren't letting me.

He closes his eyes, taking several deep breaths before he opens them.

Sadness replaces the rage so prominent moments before. When he speaks, it's like he's headed for a funeral instead of my home. "I know what I did, Aric. I know how I failed you and your mother. I feel it and grieve every day. That day in Lesoto, I watched my mate and the best man I'll ever know die. I live with the decisions I made every day." He angles his position to better see me. "Yet I still try to live. You, you're trying to die."

I swallow hard. Maybe I am.

He starts up the mountain again. A few miles pass in silence. Having stayed awake for several days, hits me all at once. I'm ready to collapse even though I'm trying not to show it.

Nothing like catching Mimi riding a bear down a path to wake me right up. She holds out a branch full of berries, using her magic to drop them into the bear's open mouth before gobbling down a few of her own.

I forget that I'm still supposed to be angry at Martin. "Did you see that?" I ask.

"Yes," he says, sounding defeated.

I cock a brow at him. "Is there something going on that I should know about?"

"Desperate times call for desperate measures," he mumbles.

"Huh?"

He drags his free hand down his suddenly very sweaty skin. "I need advice and requested Mimi's presence."

"You need advice?" I ask.

"Yes."

"You?" I repeat.

"*Yes*," he says, sounding annoyed.

I just about keel over. "From *Mimi*?" I press.

His shoulders droop. "Yes," he confesses.

I just stare at him. "How desperate are you to get advice from that lunatic?"

Misery plagues Martin's features as he turns his focus from the road back to me. "Very," he admits.

"Whoa." I hold my hands out. "Wait a minute. This isn't about me, is it?" I throw the door open, ready to leap out of the vehicle.

Martin's strong clasp to my shoulder keeps me from jumping, but it's his words that freeze me in place.

"You're failing him, Aric. That incredible Leader we were all privileged to know would be heartbroken to see what you've become."

I shut the door slowly and turn back in the direction of the road. Yeah, he would be. But knowing so doesn't soothe the monster stalking within me. The one who demands I avenge him with blood.

Chapter Two

Martin doesn't speak to me the remainder of the ride. It's just as well, I'm done talking to him. I'm done talking to everyone.

The gate opens with a whining groan. If Dad was here, he would have oiled it at the sound of the first squeak. He and I would have swept the snow lining the driveway, not allowed it to accumulate and melt in stages on its own.

Martin's SUV rocks side to side as he breaks over the top layer of ice. The path lined with evergreens and old oaks part, the house slowly coming into view as Martin nears the halfway mark of our driveway.

Our house isn't like the ones you find in the city or even just outside of town. This is the Colorado mountains. Neighbors live miles apart and dirt paths distinguish one property from the next. There's no need for gravel. Tar just poisons the air and pollutes the fragrant aroma of soil and pine. Around here, a driveway is something you mow in summer and plow through in winter.

I've done neither in a long time.

Like a veil, the trees lining the sides part, revealing the house my father built for his bride. It's mostly slate, solid like the wards surrounding it. It's big. Too big. With too many bedrooms for such a small family. My parents planned to fill it with children.

But just like their dream to grow old together, that one didn't come through either.

With a curse and a few mental kicks to the head, my attention wanders to the second level, where a set of heavy wood doors separate the terrace from the master bedroom. I take what I said back. There is one person I still talk to. Even though she never has much to say.

The sadness I beat down in exchange for rage jabs at my ribs when I realize how abandoned and unkempt everything appears. My home looks abandoned and neglected, nothing like what was once the envy of the town.

My friends have offered to help me tend to it a few times. Each time, I shut their efforts down. Hell, I've shut them down and out of my life.

Liam still calls, trying to convince me to hang out.

Koda will text, telling me to pull my head out my ass.

Gemini watches me from a distance. He'll track me every now and then, saying nothing and walking quietly behind me. He thinks it's what I need.

What I need is nothing my friends can give.

I shake my head, trying to place how things went so wrong so fast and how even my home seems to mourn.

Weeds poke through sections of snow the sun has managed to melt. They choke the once lush, sprawling lawn, spreading out to kill as much as they can. The door to Dad's woodshed hangs on one hinge. One more storm will finish it off. I try to huff with annoyance, but shame has me hanging my head.

The last time I tended to the yard was the morning Dad died. Winter came early that year and lasted longer than it should. It's no excuse. Bad weather or good, I haven't looked after the house or the property in any capacity. I don't want to. It no longer feels like home.

My dad's booming voice no longer howls for me to come in for supper. My mother doesn't chase after me, nailing me in the head with the muddy socks I left on the floor. We no longer leap from the balcony of our rear terrace as beasts to hunt beneath the star-strewn night, nor do I pad quietly inside after raising hell with my friends.

My eyes dart around, taking every inch of land, every root poking through the rough patches of dirt, and all the boulders shaded by trees as old as time. I used to race up this path following a long day at school, knowing all the love and comfort I took for granted would be waiting just inside.

Like a fool, I thought my father was unstoppable. I was convinced he'd always be here. I believed Mom would always be so full of life. God, how naïve I was to think nothing would ever change.

Home for sure isn't home anymore. It's a building belonging to two broken souls.

"Listen, Aric. Mimi wants to talk to you—"

"That's a hard pass," I say, meaning it.

"Aric, wait."

I shake off his clasp to my shoulder and hop out. "Are you out of your mind, Martin? I'll only end up pissing her off and she'll only end up cursing me. I can do without sprouting a tail on my forehead, thanks."

If he tries to say more, I don't give him a chance. I take off in a rush, shaking off some of the rage so the wards surrounding my house recognize me as family, not someone intent on harming anyone inside.

It works enough that the brush of the magic only mildly irritates me. A few years back, I'd barely feel it all. Now, I'm lucky it doesn't reduce me to dust.

The door unlatches before I reach for the handle. Slowly, it opens, welcoming me inside. "What the hell?"

Wards protect, they don't invite.

I whip around, expecting someone there, only to see Martin maneuver his vehicle back to the road.

My backpack barely makes a sound as I step inside and lower it to the floor. My jacket follows. I don't want to be tangled in my clothes if I have to *change*.

I inhale deep, taking in my surroundings and the aromas filtering through the air.

A thin layer of dust coats the wooden floors of the foyer and the staircase leading up to the second and third floor. No one's been up. No one's been down.

In the dining room to my right, a spider has begun to spin a web along the large picture window that looks out to the garden.

When Dad was alive, Mom kept the house spotless, a hard task with me traipsing in mud from all the adventures with my friends and all the clothes I dropped everywhere.

Years ago, Spring would have signaled it was time to prep the garden boxes Dad and I had built for Mom in his shed. She'd plant the vegetables first, tending to the herbs she'd start in the kitchen until they were strong enough to transfer outside.

I keep up with the house just enough to keep bugs and vermin away. The garden boxes are a mess of dead plants and rotting wood. The lawn, I don't know, maybe the deer will keep it short enough. I wish I cared. I don't. This place is nothing more than a mausoleum honoring what once was.

My frown deepens when I sense another presence. My hands ball into fists as I veer, expecting an attack. Only a view of the library greets me, the same book Dad was reading left open to the same page on his desk.

I step further inside, careful not to alert anything that might be aware of my presence. A faint scent of my mother wanders in from the kitchen. It's a few days old, which means she hasn't bothered leaving her suite since I last made her breakfast. Has she even eaten at all? I take another step forward, my keen vision sweeping over the large foyer.

Something is here. I find myself turning back to the front of the house even as I watch the door close behind me. "Mom?" I call, no longer bothering to be quiet.

She doesn't answer. I didn't expect her to, but still. I investigate the entire first floor and the cellar before jogging upstairs.

I don't bother checking my room. It's on the other side of the house. My pace slows as I head to my parents' suite. I hate seeing my mother this way. I hate watching her slowly perish. I think she's only waiting for me to graduate and then she'll leave me. Just like Dad.

She needs a reason to live.

But I can't find one to give her. I stop just outside her door, my knuckles pausing briefly before knocking. "Mom?" I whisper, wishing my voice didn't sound so weak.

"Come in, son," she says.

With as much strength as I can muster, I step inside, my heart breaking further as I approach?

Messy white sections of hair nudge through a pink blanket she's cocooned herself in. The curtains are drawn. Aside from the very small crack between the thick drapes, there's no light.

It's cold in here, more than it should be. She hasn't bothered to turn on the heat or start a fire in the hearth. In a healthy *were*, it would have to drop below zero to cause more than a minor inconvenience. But Mom is frail and thin.

I ease down beside her, my weight sinking the edge of the mattress. I want to yell at her, to tell her Dad would be disappointed in what she's become. But I'm not Martin, and I won't be cruel to her.

My hand slides over her head, smoothing the oily strands against her scalp. I force down the lump in my throat when bits of hair pull away to join the other clumps on her pillow. I meant to comfort her. All I did was cause more damage.

"You smell of blood," she says. "Yours and two others."

"Yeah," I say. I don't deny it. She knows what I do. Like Martin, she doesn't approve. I can't figure out if it's because she fears for my well-being or she's jealous I might die first.

Her brown eyes, once so alive with humor, stare blankly at the photo of her wedding day. I cock my head, noticing there's a smaller one lying beside it. The corners of it curl from handling and the harshness of time.

I lift it, surprised to find it's an old photo of me.

I can't be more than a few months old. Dad's holding me. I was supposedly a big baby, but I look tiny in Dad's strong arms. We're facing each other. I'm smiling. Dad has his head thrown back, laughing.

"He loved you fiercely," she says. She presses her dried lips tight, as if swallowing back the tears still left to fall. "Never has a father adored a child more."

I place the picture carefully back. These memories don't comfort me. Neither does Mom, given her fragility.

If her death would grant her peace maybe it'd be something I could pray for. But leaving me young and alone, and knowing I don't want her to go, peace isn't something she'll find in the afterlife.

If purgatory was something she could walk through alive, I think this would be what she's experiencing now. Not really dead and nowhere near alive.

"You should eat," I say. "For me. Okay?"

"For you," she repeats without inflection.

I reach for the full pitcher of water and fill her empty glass.

"We were blessed to have you," she says. Her voice trails as she remembers. But memories are now a curse and worsen her state.

Tears spill from her eyes, drawing lines into her pale skin. "Was it wrong to want more of you?" she asks. "Babies so sweet they'd cuddle and fall asleep against me? Little boys to chase after the way I chased after you?" She meets my eyes. "Maybe a girl to dress in pretty clothes?"

My hand clenches the glass. It won't take much to break it. It also won't take much to throw it against the wall. But I won't upset her further.

What do you want, Mom?

What can I give you to look forward to?

How can I make you happy?

I slip my arm around her back and raise her to me, pressing my lips to her forehead and wishing I could take her pain for her. The bones from her back press against my palm. She doesn't have much longer.

"Stay with me, Mama," I tell her. "I can't lose you, too."

Her shoulders tremble as she cries quietly. I hold her against me until she stops.

It takes time for her to quiet. It's okay. I let her. It's only when I think she's settled that I adjust her position in my arms and help her drink some water. She downs the entire thing, clearly dehydrated and in need of it. But instead of drinking on her own, she waited for me to give her a reason to.

Just like she's waiting for me to give her a reason to live.

"I'll get dinner started," I say.

She doesn't reply. I hurry down the stairs and out of the house, figuring to snag some trout from the nearby stream.

I hop over the terrace just to freeze when I find Mimi sitting on a stump.

"What do you want?" I ask.

She cackles. We're talking full-on evil witch; I'm going to eat your little dog cackle. "Now is this any way to treat an old friend, boy?"

"Old friend?" I ask. Like most *weres*, I've spent my life avoiding her. Nothing good has ever come from cozying up to Mimi. "I think you have the wrong wolf."

She responds with a wide, semi-toothy grin. Yup. This hag is psycho.

"Do I?" she asks. She cocks her head, her beady eyes shimmering with malice and enough crazy to give me pause. "Oh, that's right. You don't remember." She cackles again. "This could be part of the problem."

I don't like games and I'm in no mood to play. "What problem?"

She twiddles her fingers, the motions growing frantic as her thoughts overtake her.

I jump up when the mirror image of me appears and *changes*, becoming my wolf and tearing into a werehyena that leaps from the brush.

I know this hyena. I encountered him in Mafeteng.

His back strikes the tree to my right, bringing it down from the force of my charge. I start toward the illusion of him and of me, the roar and temptation of battle calling me forth.

I stop in my tracks. Mimi is screwing with me. This *were* protected the witch who murdered my father. A witch that no one had ever challenged and lived. Mimi isn't simply pulling things from midair. She's pulling my memories, showing me what I did.

Once grown, most *weres* range between four and six hundred pounds in their animal form. This hyena teetered close to the latter, where I remain close to the former. But what he had in muscle and brute strength, I made up for in speed and anger.

His fangs find my throat, cutting through the muscle and severing my jugular. Like a fountain, my blood spews onto his spotted face and blinds us both.

He almost had me. He would have taken me out. But my claws, and my commitment to avenge my father, wouldn't allow it. I broke his ribcage wide open and sank my fangs through his heart.

I cup my throat as the image of me *changes* back to my human form. The pressure I add doesn't help me like it did then. As I watch, the healing power of my wolf knits the surrounding tissue closed and slows the blood soaking my chest.

My hand falls away as I take in my kill, just as I did that day. I should have sat and rested my beaten form, given how my wolf worked overtime to save me. Instead, I kicked over the hyena's carcass and watched him *change* back to human. Even in death, my pride wouldn't allow him to see me weak.

His limbs quiver as the last of his lifeline trickles along the muddy ground. His chest is wide open. There's nothing left of his hyena spirit to heal him. Even if there was, the damage I inflicted was far beyond his ability.

In human form, he was tall and lean; very unlike the formidable beast he became. His soles were deeply calloused for a *were*. This was someone used to walking down stony paths and rough terrain barefoot.

I tilt his chin up with my foot. He died with his eyes wide opened. He hadn't expected me to beat him. I proved him wrong, just as I had his spell-wielding mistress. She was my first kill, and the one who had mattered the most.

I thought killing the witch responsible for my father's death would bring me a sense of accomplishment, maybe even an inkling of peace. All it did was make me lust after evil, to bring it down so no one would ever hurt like we have.

A mournful cry fills my surroundings as the rushing wind breaks through the trees and cools my skin. The hyena's woman appears, clutching a child against her chest. She throws herself on top of her dead mate, burying her face against his, as the little girl she holds whimpers in fear.

I watch the image of me stagger away from her, dizzy from the amount of blood I lost. My dark brown hair is red from the carnage, the longer length on top, plastered against my forehead.

Blood and death come with battle. That's okay with me. What I don't like is how my light brown eyes fire with that lust to kill as they take in the woman and her child.

I take a step back, not liking what I see now. But that other me? The me then. He watches them for a long time, licking his lips as if he can already taste them.

CHAPTER THREE

The image fades away. I allowed the woman and child to live, but only just barely.

"Did you know he only worked for the witch to spare and help his family?" Mimi asks.

"Did *you* know how many women and children he brought to her to kill? How many *he* killed for her?" I counter.

Mimi laughs. She's having fun. I'm not. "No," she admits. "But his wife and child were just innocent little doves, weren't they? Cute little things you yearned to slaughter."

I don't argue, hating the disgust that roils my stomach. I shove it down with more rage.

"What do you want, Mimi? Are you here to haunt me? Do you have some twisted need to make me relive each one of my kills?" I cross my arms. "Go, ahead. Everything I did was just and within our laws. Do your worst."

Her grin widens enough to show the gray color along her gumline and the few teeth still hanging on for dear life.

Like an idiot, I challenged her to do her worst. I'll give it to Mimi, she doesn't disappoint.

I'm back inside my house, just outside my parent's suite. The hall is dark. I didn't bother to switch on the chandelier that my grandparents gifted Mom and Dad on their wedding day.

We rarely bother with lights anymore. It doesn't change anything. There's only darkness with Dad gone. He no longer whistles as he leaves his suite, ready to start his day. No longer laughs hard enough to shake the walls.

Quiet has silenced his tune as well as his booming laughter. And his strength, the glue that made us all one? Yeah, that left us, too.

With his absence the silence is more pronounced, and the melancholy is as loud as any mournful word. Still, that's not what I focus on. Not with Mom crying as hard as she is in this memory.

Rain splatters against the stained-glass window overlooking the foyer. The raindrops start slow, a staccato of pitter patters that gain momentum with each wretched sob my mother unleashes. She's in agony, the force of her broken heart more painful than any blow I ever gave.

This wasn't the day we found out my father was dead. It wasn't even the day of his service. It was mere days before I left on this last mission, her mourning as raw as the moment we felt him leave this earth.

Instead of rushing in to comfort her, to tell her that I hurt, too, and that no matter what, we still have each other—instead of simply being *present*, I take a seat outside the door like a coward.

One leg is bent against my chest, the other leg is stretched out motionless. My stare is blank. There are no tears, just all the ugly that comes with being weak.

Weak. That's what I am when it comes to my mother. It's pathetic, especially since hope is what she needs.

I find enough muscle to stand and stagger in the direction of my room, leaving my mother alone. I stop in place when her voice screams through the door. "Why did you leave me, Aidan? I can't make it on my own."

My breath releases hard enough to rattle my chest. My mother feels abandoned. As I watch myself walk away, I can't deny she's wrong.

The image fades as fluidly as it arrives. Mimi is known for cruelty. I never experienced it firsthand until now. I round on her, yelling at the top of my lungs. "What's your problem?"

"I don't have a problem. You do." She jumps off the log, her ragged cloak flapping as she levitates toward me.

"Oh, yeah? And what's that?" I snarl.

"Hmm, how can I put it?" She holds up a crooked finger. "Oh, I know. You're an asshole."

"*What*?" I jab my finger at her. "You come on my land—unwelcomed and unwanted—showing me things you shouldn't be showing me and insult me like *I'm* the wacko?"

Light explodes in front of me and another image of me appears. It's brief but it's enough.

Liam is chasing after me, telling me to wait. He reaches for me and tries to place his arm around my shoulder. I shove him harder than I should, knocking him to the ground and leaving him winded. Koda rushes forward, growling, and ready to punch me square in the face for hurting our friend.

If not for Gemini and his twin wolf, holding him back, Koda and me would have come to blows. I reward Gemini's effort with a stiff middle finger and a not-so polite request for all of them to fuck off.

Mimi nods at the image as it fades. "I take it back. You're a rude *and* selfish asshole."

I loom over her, bordering on violence, and she just squints at me. I start to tell her to take a flying leap when I realize I can't speak, or move, or….

Great, she just hexed me, and I just let her. I glance down at my navel. No fangs are puncturing through my shirt. Not yet. I still have all of my toes, I think. But that's about all I can say.

Mimi reaches inside her cloak sleeve. She pulls out a porcelain cup with a giant yellow rose at its center filled to the brim with steaming tea.

She eyes me up and down.

"Hmm," she says. "This might be worse than I thought."

She levitates back and forth, pondering things a hag probably shouldn't ponder. This is fantastic. I'm supposed to be getting Mom dinner. Instead, I'm frozen stiff with a maniacal witch contemplating ways to torture me.

I focus hard, managing to make my hand move just a little. Mimi takes a sip of her tea and slaps the back of my hand hard enough to sting yet steady enough not to spill a drop from her cup.

"Stop it," she says. "I won't tolerate any distractions." She pauses, beaming and pointing. "Distraction. That's what you need, and I know just the gal to do the distracting!"

My features sour. *A girl, really?* I think back to the female at the airport with the glittery sign. *Good luck with that one.*

She throws back her head, cackling like she heard me, but then it's like the common sense she lacks jars the humor right out of her.

"No. Mustn't toy with the space-time continuum. No, no, no. Magic doesn't like that. Perfect balance and all." She resumes her levitated pacing but only manages a few strides. "Unless it's brief and for the benefit of good," she reasons.

"Huh?"

She does a little dance. Odd, seeing she's one bad levitation away from a broken hip. "The world needs her," she insists. She stops dancing, appearing sad. "She just doesn't know how much, yet."

"What the hell are you talking about?" I snap, shocking me and Mimi by managing to talk.

She pats my face a few times, giddy and evidently impressed. "You are a strong one, Aric Connor. Yes, you are."

My voice slurs as Mimi adds another dose of mojo. "What are you talking about?" I repeat.

"Not what, *whom*," she replies. She frowns. "The dark ones like her."

"Who?" I mumble. This hag is on my last nerve.

Mimi continues as if uninterrupted. "Like her to hurt. Like her to suffer." She frowns. "They torture her. Play with her until they can get her good and dead."

I don't get a good look at Mimi as she turns away, but for the briefest second, I catch the worry deepening the creases of her face.

She returns her empty teacup back into her sleeve and reaches deep into her other sleeve. She sticks her tongue out as she fidgets through the interior, her face perking up when she seems to find what she's looking for. It takes some finagling, but she yanks out a broken staff the length of her body.

Mimi lifts the staff triumphantly in the air. "This used to belong to Gandalf," she says.

"Really?" I ask.

"Of course not. Gandalf isn't real." She stabs the pointy end into the ground. "Asshole," she mutters as an afterthought.

The slur isn't enough to make her lose her focus. She gets to work, dragging the stick into the ground as she hovers back and forth.

It takes some doing, but I manage to wrench my head enough to see the scratch marks she makes.

Four long lines run parallel in equal length. The first two, she connects with small lines in between, similar to a train track, the exception being the lines are slanted and don't extend past the borders.

She repeats the motion, her frown deepening when she reaches the end of the second set of parallel lines. "Now, where are you?" Mimi asks. She stamps her little feet; her orthopedic shoes making small indentations into the ground despite that she's still levitating. "Don't hide her from me. Not when she needs him. Not with how badly the world needs *her*." Her voice softens and I almost don't catch what Mimi says. "And not when he needs her more."

I attempt to holler at her, but Mimi's spell makes my words come out in slow motion. "I don't need anyone."

Mimi ignores me, the speed as she levitates increasing as she sweeps back and forth, inspecting her work. It's then I realize she's drawing ley lines.

Dad explained ley lines a long time ago. They're magical networks that run along the earth in conjunction with fault lines. They're what keep time and reality moving forward. Witches and oracles often draw them out when they're attempting to predict the future. It's permitted, but exceptionally hard spell work to master. What's not permitted is to mess with time, past or present. That's dangerous, as in, End of Days, dangerous.

No worries. Only a lunatic would....

Mimi scratches in a few more marks.

Oh, no.

"Are you nuts?" I slur.

"We prefer the term mentally unstable," she replies.

And then she cackles, because she hasn't proved she's insane enough.

"Mimi, *don't.*" She ignores me, feverishly sketching runes along either side. The tips spark and sizzle, smoking and melting away the surrounding snow and singeing the ground.

Worms and bugs slither through the blackened earth, crawling and skittering frantically away.

My eyes widen. "Whatever you're doing, stop it now."

Of course, she doesn't. Why would she when I sound like a drooling idiot? I try harder, adding will to my voice to push through her hex. "I, Aric Connor, pureblood Leader and future alpha order you to—"

"Ah, shad up," Mimi mutters. "I need to focus. Evil wants her dead. Good needs her alive. That's my story and I'm stickin' to it."

"You're risking unleashing the apocalypse or some other crazy to save one girl?"

"And a weird one at that," Mimi agrees. She shrugs. "What can I do, life as we know it won't go on without her."

"Who?" I demand. "What girl is so special everything will die without her?"

"I never said we're going to die," she replies. "Don't be so dramatic."

"Oh, good," I say.

"It's more like the power of darkness will overtake us, force us to feast on our eyeballs until evil finishes us off and wears our remains like jewelry," she adds.

"*What*?" I spit out. "Mimi, this isn't a joke. What exactly are you trying to do here?"

She waves me off with a bat of her hand. "You'll know when you need to and forget when you have to."

I was wrong. Mimi isn't crazy.

Crazy is too soft a word.

I writhe back and forth, trying to break through the last few layers of her hex.

Mimi ignores my efforts, focusing on the lines she constructed in the dirt. She taps her finger against her long chin, mumbling to herself.

"I'll kill us," she says. "I'll blow us all to oblivion if I mess this thing up."

"No kidding," I say in that same, slow-mo way.

"Our intestines will shoot out from our groins wrapped like bows around our hair."

"Mimi!"

Mimi shakes her head. "And it just gets merrier from there."

"Then stop!" I yell. "For the love of all, Mimi, don't—"

"Unless, I get lucky. *Really* lucky." She gives it some thought. "Never mind, we're all gonna die."

I stop moving. "If you're trying to make me feel better, it's not working, hag."

She pauses, her neck making an odd creaking noise when she turns her attention back to me. In a rush of gray smoke, Mimi pounces and yanks a few hairs clean off my scalp.

"Ow!" I growl.

She eyes the strands pieces like a precious trophy. "That should do it," she says.

She returns to the first line, starting from the beginning, sprinkling my hair as she hovers. "Evil is eating away at the tigress and those she most loves." Like an old-time cartoon, a light bulb appears over Mimi's head and flickers on. "And when darkness tips the scales in its favor, light is needed to even the odds."

The smoke clears and the ley lines Mimi drew become nothing more than etchings in the earth. I all but keel over with relief. Still, I can't let this go. Dad wouldn't.

I humor her, trying to get a sense of what she's up to before I pounce. "Right," I agree. "You're always right. But what does that have to do with me?"

Mimi's smile is so full of wicked glee I'm certain she only spared me just to eat me. "It means to come out of your darkness, you must become her light. Only then will you vanquish her torment and yours."

The rows of ley lines spark to life with a sinister gray glow. Birds take flight from their nests, screaming. I don't mean they chirp or caw. I mean they shriek like children running from a clown with red balloons.

Frogs and crickets bounce by me, snakes emerge from holes, racing past them.

This doesn't look good. It looks bad, super bad. Nuclear bomb bad.

Mimi jumps in place, clapping her hands and evidently awed by her spell work.

"It's time, Aric Connor," she says. "Find her. Save her. And perhaps you'll save yourself." She points at me. "But do so quickly or both of you will die. She in her time, and you in yours."

The hex shatters and I'm free. But it's not Mimi's doing. Uh-uh. These ley lines are killing all the magic around us, including Mimi's.

The ley lines build with power and energy. I back away, every instinct bent on staying alive taking over. My eyes dart toward the house. I have to get Mom out of here.

"Even if you reach her in time, Eliza won't go with you," Mimi says. "She's willing to die. Are you willing to let her?"

"Enough of your manipulative bullshit," I snap. "Tell me who I have to save."

Mimi clasps her hands together, her voice quieting. "The one you'll always love."

"My mom?" I guess.

Mimi's face falls. She doesn't call me an asshole. Not this time. But she's definitely thinking it.

"Aren't you listening, boy? You'll know when you need to and forget when you have to."

"Why?" I question.

Mimi presses her lips tight, that same sad expression I thought I saw earlier flickering across her beady eyes. "It's not time for you to stay. It's only time to heal and save so she may fulfill her purpose."

She's not making sense and it's pissing me off. I stalk forward, ready to rip her a new one. I manage to reach the stump when her spell work explodes, knocking Mimi across the yard and right out of her orthopedic shoes. Her feet quiver and her support hose smokes.

I start toward her, thinking she's dead, only for my steps to lighten and my surroundings to fade away. I lift my hands, watching them disappear as I vanish in a haze of gray.

Chapter Four

I'm floating. Clouds of white encasing me and lulling my muscles to relax until I fall limp.

Mimi killed me. Killed us both. It's okay. After all the stupid decisions I made and all the suicide missions I went on, death was coming anyway. I just never thought I'd find it in Mimi's twisted hands.

It's just my time, I guess.

No.

Never mind.

I take it back.

While death is something I often begged for, I never sought it at my own hands. But the chances I took, and the monsters I hunted, could have yielded the same results.

Disappointment in myself stirs from deep in my gut. It's not an emotion I expected, not now. I hate the truth of it and how it burns its way to my chest. I do my best to dismiss such a useless emotion, concentrating on the white light beckoning me closer.

It doesn't work. Regret joins my disappointment, swirling and making it hard to breathe, even as I venture closer to what I'm certain is ultimate peace.

Sadness and shame follow, growing stronger.

I never said goodbye to Mom. I hate myself for it. I wallow in grief, knowing when she realizes I'm gone, she'll join me, too. It's wrong. She held in this long only for me to let her down.

The clouds burst open and only light remains, blinding me the faster I plummet.

"Dad?" I call out. "Dad, I'm coming. Are you there?"

Please, tell me you're with me.

My eyes burn, not just in anticipation of seeing Dad, but who I won't see for a long, *long* time.

Gemini. He was my patience when I had none to give. Another brain to help me strategize and reason through the unreasonable. He didn't speak a word of English when we met, but he always knew how to be the perfect friend.

Koda. He thinks he's a burden. He doesn't yet see the hero within. He always had my back. Except when I was wrong. When I messed up, he was honest, holding me to a higher standard than I deserved.

Liam. No filter. Brutally honest. All heart. All he ever wanted was to have fun and maybe change the world for the better. He changed my world just by being a part of my life.

My friends. Will they forgive me for wronging them? I hope so. They deserved much more than I was.

The light brightens, threatening to burn through my retinas. I close them tight. I'm almost there. It's almost time.

Torment. Why do I feel it when my father is so close?

So, what if I never became the alpha my kind expected?

So, what if I didn't lead my pack as Guardians of the Earth?

Does it matter that I didn't pass on my knowledge and skills?

No. There'll be others.

I killed those who needed killing.

I avenged my father's death.

And now, I shall walk beside him forever.

I don't a need a wife.

I don't need to carry on the Connor name.

I just need to come home.

A cold breeze sweeps over my face and the intensity of the light lessens, revealing only a sparkling white beauty below.

I'm here, Papa. I'm home.

I slam face first into a mound of frozen snow, shattering my nose.

I cough, spitting out sand, salt, and snow. "*What the hell?*"

The sudden cacophony of noise overwhelms my senses. I push up on my arms, growling and cursing Mimi for all she's worth. Nope, I'm not joining Dad. That hag has other plans.

The small bones in my nose slide back into place with a snap along with my fractured knee. It hurts. The cold from the pile of snow I'm half-buried in adding another layer of ache.

With more grace than I landed, I scramble out, taking a moment to wash the blood from my mouth and face with fresh snow.

Cars speed past me, blasting their speakers. Metallica's *Seek and Destroy* competes with Springsteen's *Cadillac Ranch* and... *Rudolph the Red Nose Reindeer*?

Spring just started. What's up with the Christmas music?

I look up. An arc of red and green lights flash against Santa as he waves from his plastic sleigh.

Is this a joke? Am I in hell?

I swipe at my face with the back of my hand. All that does is smear more blood across my cheek. My skin burns from my colossal landing, and I shiver from the abrupt change in temperature.

Colorado was maybe thirty or so degrees. Here, wherever here is, borders close to zero.

I'm not in a city. At least, not a large one. It's a suburb of sorts, based on the size of the hospital just a few yards from where I landed.

The campus isn't huge, neither is the parking deck. I take in where the community hospital starts and ends. Everything in the vicinity, down to the neighboring homes, reinforce my beliefs that this isn't some grand metropolis. But why did I land here?

More vehicles speed by me. I catch sight of their license plates and just about hurtle myself into oncoming traffic.

No.

I whip around, inspecting the plates on each car in the lot to make certain.

I'm not in hell.

But it's a close second.

I'm in New Jersey!

Of all the places Mimi could have sent me.

I return my attention to the lot, trying to get a sense on why I was specifically dropped near a hospital.

Garland covered lampposts with large wreaths and candy canes secured to their centers illuminate my surroundings. The bright obnoxious lighting from the dirty bulbs guides the medical staff exiting the building and gives them a false sense of safety. They make their way toward their vehicles, oblivious to creatures my kind kills on their behalf.

Some workers move swiftly, burrowing deep into their coats when the wind picks up and fresh fallen snow sails across the lot. Others, although cold, shuffle slowly, evidently having experienced one monster of a shift.

I scan the group and the next few after that. Is she here? The female I'm supposed to help or whatever? Mimi called her a girl. I take it she's young. Maybe she's an aid or cleaning person.

Or maybe I'm just in the wrong place.

I rub my bare arms, calling forth my wolf to warm me. He takes his time, still shocked like me to find us here. My short black T-shirt, jeans, and hiking boots were good enough for thirty-degree weather, not so much for this.

Not one person who leaves the building holds my attention, neither do the few visitors who straggle toward the deck. A couple stops short halfway to the gate just to argue. She pushes him and walks away. He curses under his breath and leaves in the opposite direction. I eye them closely, but I don't feel a need to chase her down, nor do I sense that she's in immediate danger.

The sky deepens from an ashy gray to jet black, dropping the temp a few more degrees. I glance around, waiting for anything that may clue me in on how to track this girl.

It was morning when I arrived in Colorado. It was also spring. It's evening here and the time of year when the sun sets sooner.

The bitterness I've grown used to coats my tongue. Being out here is giving me too much time to think. Why does it have to be Christmas? I barely survived the last few holidays. I'd prefer not to push through another one in a place I don't belong.

I kick at the snow edging the walkway as a young woman steps out from the building alone. I perk up, thinking she may be the one.

She waves to a driver parked illegally. The engine roars and the woman hurries inside.

A growl escapes my throat as my frustration grows. Where exactly am I supposed to go? I take a sniff, hoping to pick up on anything unusual that may help me track down the girl.

Footsteps approach behind me, human ones that keep an odd pace.

My muscles tense. There's something off about him.

A male with more hair on his face than on his head takes a drag from a long cigarette. His eyes glassy and his expression lost. "ER's just ahead, man. You're almost there."

"*What?*"

He staggers forward, too high to run away, but not high enough to realize I'm dangerous.

"Tell them you were hit by a car." He smacks at the crook of his arm. "They'll start the IV there. When they're not looking run. My boy Roz will meet you East Main and Mechanic."

"I don't need you or your friend," I growl. "What *you* need is to do better, human. My kind aren't risking their hides just for you to throw your life away."

It's a stupid remark to make. Humans who aren't mated to *weres* are ignorant to vamps, witches, and us. Still, that rage that's more friend than foe pokes through, permitting me to say what I do.

He nods, even though he doesn't understand. With a shaky hand he takes another drag, giving me plenty of space as he makes his way down the walkway.

In his wake the breeze picks up and the sky spits out the first few flakes. It doesn't take much for the moisture in the air to shift and the flurries to thicken and fall faster. I shove my hands into my pockets when the wind pricks at my wet skin. It's going to be a long, cold night. I need to find this girl fast.

I think back to what Mimi said, wondering if I missed something important. The addict reaches the opening to the Emergency Department. I shake my head. Please don't tell me I need this guy to get to her. Whoever she's supposed to be.

The male disappears beneath the bright red sign as the light switches ahead and more cars speed by. This time, the Scorpion's *Rock You Like a Hurricane* goes head-to-head with Bon Jovi's *Blood on Blood* and the most annoying song ever made, *Dominic the Donkey.*

The snowflakes become denser, making it hard to see far ahead. I'm not sure where I'm headed. I just know I can't keep standing here.

I start toward the row of homes in the opposite direction of the hospital. Maybe the girl lives close by and Mimi has terrible aim. But as soon as I turn, an unnerving energy stops me, and I can't take another step.

My wolf comes to life, encouraging me back in the direction of the hospital and toward the bright letters of the emergency department. I listen, calling upon him to warm me some more.

With the energy my wolf is using to keep me from freezing, my need to eat accelerates. How I'll eat is a different story. It shouldn't shock me Mimi dropped me far away from my wallet and into a dirty pile of snow. I suppose I should be grateful that I didn't land on the walkway with a bag full of stolen money laying on my chest. That crazy hag would pull something like that.

I pause, thinking about how Mimi appeared when we were blown into oblivion. If she's dead, does that mean I'm stuck here, in this time? I think through her last few words. No. My time is limited. Just enough to help her and maybe myself.

"Nice fuckin' coat, dipshit!" one of the state's classiest residents calls out, this one blasting enough techno trash to split his POS car in half.

I don't need reminding I'm not wearing a coat. It takes everything I have not to chase him down and pound the sarcasm out of him.

I'm halfway to the emergency room when my head shoots in the direction of the quiet lot. My muscles tense and my wolf releases a growl. Another predator is near, warning me to keep my distance.

This isn't my turf. I get it. But I'm not leaving until I accomplish my mission and this other preternatural will respect that.

I double-back, scanning the area for any subtle movement. The feel of danger surges. I try to fix on the exact location except the falling snow is too dense for me to catch more than the aroma of nesting squirrels, the lingering trail of a few pedestrians, and the acidic smell of roaring mufflers.

For a moment, I think this predator is further away, watching me from a distance, readying to attack. As I near the spot where I landed, the threat from that other monster shoves me more aggressively, cautioning me to stay away or else.

"Or else what?" I rumble.

I frown, waiting for an attack that doesn't come.

I advance cautiously forward, my fists clenching in anticipation of a fight. This predator should know better than to fight me in public. The hospital and nearby neighborhoods are full of witnesses who'll recognize our supernatural speed and strength, even in our human forms. Ideally, we should settle our beef somewhere more private. Except while this area isn't a booming city, it's not exactly secluded.

My gaze shifts. A few blocks away, there's a small park. The trees surrounding it should provide enough coverage so I can take down this cat.

Cat?

I take in a deep breath. Yeah, I definitely sense an undercurrent of jungle aroma that accompanies big cats.

More out of instinct than anything else, I pivot, walking backwards. A young woman in a sleek navy running jacket and pants walks out of a side exit and into the lot. She adjusts the drawstring backpack strapped to her back, unaware of a male who shadows her closely.

I adjust my position, walking parallel to them and keeping them in my periphery. I'm not far and with the sidewalk elevated to the lot, I have a decent vantage point.

My brows furrow. I'm unsure why I follow. Not right away. But it doesn't take me long to figure it out.

The male increases his stride, digging his hands deep into the black coat covering his green surgical scrubs. The female's hips sway back and forth seductively. I don't think it's intentional. The male seems to think otherwise.

A small grin cuts along his face as his gaze drinks in her body. He likes what he sees. I beat back the disgust turning my stomach. At best, she's barely legal and although he's young, he's too old to desire someone her age.

This male deserves a good smack upside the head and a better dose of decency. He's pathetic and can't possibly be the threat I sense. What alerts my wolf is formidable. Lusting after someone her age makes this idiot weak and classifies him as a different type of predator.

The female slows her pace and glances in my direction. I keep my attention ahead. Eye contact will only reinforce her suspicion that I'm watching her.

The male hurries forward. He doesn't want her to escape. This is the opening he's waited for. Instead of turning around and facing her stalker, she eyes me up. I'm almost to the pile of snow Mimi body slammed me into and am running out of walk-way. This female isn't my charge. But she's become my business. I'll have to temporarily abandon my task to save her.

"Celia," the male calls out.

The name stops me dead. She turns, addressing the male.

No. Something isn't right.

Screw it.

I hop down the incline and head toward them, landing quietly between two cars and keeping close to the shadows.

"Do you need a ride?" the male asks.

"Ah, no, Dr. Bantam," she replies. Her voice is raspy and more of an alto. Odd, seeing how she's maybe five-feet-two at best. That said, she's no weakling. Her skintight running pants cover lean muscles used to running long distances, and the white stripes of her jacket lessens the definition in her arms. Her curves are pronounced, adding allure to what is otherwise a thin, athletic frame.

I notice her figure plenty, as well as her beauty. The male does too, only not the way I do. He takes her in as if naked, instead of fully dressed.

"You sure?" he asks. "You might enjoy the company." He laughs. "Every time I see you, you're by yourself."

Her voice trails as she looks in my direction. "I'm fine. Go home," she tells him.

I plaster myself against a run-down minivan, ignoring the sheet of snow that slides along the side and onto my back. The strange beast I sense is prowling closer, alerting me he's ready to fight.

He's almost upon us. Hell. Has he come for her?

My senses extend across the perimeter. If he's after this young woman, that pissant doctor will complicate matters. I could knock him out, to keep him from witnessing the fight that's about to go down, and also for being a prick.

Two birds, one stone.

The thought cuts a wolfish grin across my face. It vanishes as the female whips her head in my direction and locks her gaze on mine.

Jade green tiger eyes replace her human gaze.

My knuckles crunch as I push away from the van.

The predator isn't here for her.

The predator *is her*.

Chapter Five

"Celia?" the male says. "What's wrong? Look, I know it's late. It's been a long day for both of us. Why don't I take you to dinner? We can kickback, have a few drinks."

The female shoots her hand out, keeping the oblivious human in place when he inches forward. "There's something here." She hones in on where I wait. "You need to go."

I stalk out from the darkness. "She's right," I say. I jerk my head to the side. "Get going, Doc."

"Who are you?" the male demands. He chokes on the last word when I unleash a deadly growl.

The female replies with a challenging growl of her own. The timbre only slightly lighter. For such a small female, her growl is heady. She tosses her pack aside and storms forward, her steps barely perceptible in her rage.

"Oh, honey, you're messing with the wrong wolf," I snarl. "You want to fight? Let's go."

Mimi's raggedy and irritated voice echoes around us, scattering snow in all directions and stopping me dead. "For Hera's sake!" she crows.

Lightening cracks and the world ignites in a brilliant ball of light.

I'm thrown backward into the same pile of snow where I initially landed. My breath leaves in a harsh rush when the female crashes on top of me. I blink, clearing the spots dancing in my vision and trying to grasp what happened.

The female groans. I shift into attack mode only to be bowled over by a tundra of warmth that floods me with voracious desire.

The female jolts. Her wet curly hair bats against my cheek in her rush to sit up.

This is where I would normally strike and take control of my opponent. She weighs nothing, it'll be easy. One shift of my hips will knock her off balance. I'll hook my arm behind hers and twist. She'll be face down in the snow and I'll be the one on top. It's what I should do, how I'm trained to respond, except her touch—I don't know—it does *something* to me.

Instead of asserting my dominance, I merely watch her large eyes widen in disbelief. The snowflakes sticking to her thick lashes melt, falling in droplets to wet my face.

And still, I do nothing.

I should be raging, fighting against the spell she's trapped me in. All I do is lift my hand and trail my fingertips down her face. "You're beautiful," I whisper.

The female jerks free of my touch. She pulls back her fist and stops.

Everything simply stops.

The warmth surges, cocooning us and slapping the cold away.

I tremble, amazed how easily she soothes my beast.

Peace.

It's her gift to me, pushing away the anger and pain until only devotion remains.

I reach for her. She doesn't fight me, her bewilderment transforming to fear. I cup her face, lifting to kiss her full lips.

"Celia," I rasp.

She pulls away clasping her mouth.

She knows me.

Just as I know her.

Memories of finding her in a different place and time pummel me like saltwater against a damaged and forgotten shore.

I remember her in my bed, how she slept clutched against me, and my silent vow to always love her.

I remember kissing her. Kissing her a lot.

And how hard my friends and I fought to keep her safe, only to have her save us in return.

I swore she would always be mine.

And then she was gone.

"*Celia*," I say, again. In that single word, I plead for her to remember me.

Her eyes are wild, and fear rocks her petite frame. She tries to scramble away. I hold tight to her waist. "It's me," I tell her. "Aric."

She shakes her head, anguish crushing her sweet features. She remembers me and everything we were forced to forget. It scares her.

Hell, it scares *me*.

We weren't supposed to meet the way that we did. Mimi said it wasn't our time, that the world will need us when the moment is right.

No, this isn't our time.

Not yet.

But she's here and so am I.

I jerk upright, digging my fingers through her hair and pressing her mouth against mine.

A brief gasp catches in her chest, but not much more. She responds with equal force, the way her hands glide along my back, promising to never let me go.

My hands yank her closer, dragging up her spine to bury my fingers in her mound of wet curls. I can't get enough of her. Ecstasy consumes us and our surroundings fade away.

Celia's lips feather over mine. "Aric," she moans between breaths. "*My* Aric."

Yours. Just as you'll always be mine.

I don't tell her as much in words. I show her. My passion for her, and my time without her, spurring a lust that awakens like a caged beast.

The kisses we first shared, back when we were fifteen and naive to the heartbreak that comes with first love, were sweet, overwhelming, and awesome in all their innocence.

This kiss is nothing like the ones we exchanged all those years ago. Longing replaces sweet, and need devours any semblance of innocence.

I groan, pulling her closer, only to laugh when she responds with a purr.

Celia breaks our kiss, hurrying to stand. I kip up to my feet, reaching for her hand so she can't get too far.

She shakes her free hand as she giggles. "I'm sorry," she says. "I don't know where that came from."

My voice is unusually gravelly. "I think I do," I reply.

She stills, her gaze searching mine as she wrestles with how to respond.

A deep shade of red overtakes the soft pink coloring her cheeks. Her shyness is my undoing. "I miss that blush," I tell her, my sincerity softening my voice. "I don't know how I've survived without it."

She lifts up on her toes and strokes my cheek so gently, I almost don't feel it. It's more than I deserve after all the shit I've done. Would she run from me if she knew the torment I've inflicted since I last held her?

"You forgot about me, didn't you?" She eases back down to plant her feet, the weight of her sadness trickling into her voice. "Just like I somehow forget about you."

The manner she bites at her bottom lip destroys me. She's trying not to cry but her glistening eyes demonstrate the depth of her misery.

"You're not here for me, are you?" She sighs when I don't respond. "I take it the world isn't ready for us yet?"

"No. Not yet," I admit.

My words only worsen her unease. I hate the pain that claims her—that claims me. No, this isn't our time.

But I am here for her, and I'm not ready to let her go.

Every emotion that claws my heart can only be soothed by her touch. Using more patience than I possess, I draw her to me, lifting her chin to kiss her once more.

Our kiss deepens, turning my insides in all the best ways. Celia doesn't purr this time. A luscious whimper mixed with the tinniest of groans vibrate against my chest and heads south.

Something is very different since the last time we were together. I feel it in every part of the male I've become. I don't have a lot of experience. What I do have comes solely from my brief time with Celia. What we shared was sacred and loving. What we share now is more akin to the adult mates we are.

The need to rid myself of my clothes *and* hers overtakes me. I reach for the front zipper of her jacket when the other male's voice reminds where we are and that we're not alone.

"Celia?" he presses, his tone off.

Celia edges away from me. I follow, quick on my feet and just as fast to snatch her waist and press her back against my chest. The thick clumps of snow falling from the sky thin, morphing to an icier more dangerous blend. It melts against my dark hair as I nibble on her neck.

That male, the doctor, doesn't move, sheer indignation cementing him in place. "What happened?" he demands, his confusion adding to his resentment. "There was thunder and what sounded like a bomb exploding." He regards me like I have no business anywhere near Celia. "Who are you?"

He's challenging me in his own pathetic way. I almost laugh. He's as much of a threat to me as the snowflakes clinging to Celia's beanie. Still, humor isn't what lures my beast closer to the surface.

We don't like the way he's watching Celia. This isn't a man trying to keep his young coworker from harm. No, this is something else.

"Um, this is Aric, Dr. Bantam," she stammers. She glances up at me, trying to figure out what to say. "My, uh, boyfriend."

"Boyfriend?" I grin. "Sweetness, we both know I'm a lot more than that."

"No kidding," the male mutters under his breath.

Celia's body temperature surges, adding another few coats of red to her already scorching face. I'm not embarrassed by what he says. What sets me off is how he intends it as a slight against Celia.

My wolf thinks we should just kill him and kick his remains down the sewer. Can't this idiot see Celia belongs to us?

He shoots me a glare. Cute. His position and status may give him an edge in his workplace, but I'm the alpha here.

All I have to do to get him to submit is take a step forward. It's easy. He knows he's weaker. The thing is, he's pushing his limits when it comes to Celia.

The aroma of jealousy permeates through the doctor's skin when Celia clutches my arm. He isn't a good man. If he was, he wouldn't try for someone as young as Celia who has so much to prove.

He thinks he can do anything to her and get away with it. That makes him prey. I move on him. He takes a step back, the assertive posturing he attempts to assume, dwindling. The human populace may be unaware of supernaturals like me, but even a dipshit like him recognizes a dangerous being when he sees one.

He jerks his chin, attempting to hide his cowardice even though I can taste it.

My muscles tighten, readying to defend what's mine. *You don't get to have her and you sure as fuck won't hurt her.*

Celia's clutch to my arm tightens. "Dr. Bantam is a surgical resident," she says, speaking quickly. "He's conducting his OB rotation on my unit."

I tuck Celia against me and continue forward, hellbent on knocking his teeth in. "That's nice," I say, not meaning it.

Celia digs her heels into the snow, attempting to hold me back. I only stop because she wants me to. "Aric, you can't kill him," she urges.

She's trying to be quiet, but her frantic attempts to calm me make her loud enough to be heard.

Doc throws his hands up in surrender. "Whoa there, buddy. I don't want any trouble."

The rage I'm familiar with sets in when I catch sight of the wedding band on his finger. I stomp forward. He hurries further back. Celia squeezes me tighter.

"I'm not your buddy," I snap at him. "And you're the one asking for trouble."

"I don't know—"

I cut him off. "What are you doing going after someone too young and good for you?" I demand. "You have a wife waiting on your sorry ass to come home."

"What?" he asks. He jerks his head toward Celia. "I was just trying to be nice."

"*Aric,*" Celia warns.

She thinks I'll stop. Nope. I'm just getting started.

"Nice?" I ask, shadowing him like he shadowed Celia. "You're making moves on someone you think is an easy target."

"*What?*" His face reddens. He's not embarrassed about what he's done. He's angry that I see right through him. "That's absurd."

"Is it?" I ask.

He backs into the side of a truck. I'm close enough that I catch the barest aroma of an infant. His infant.

"You have a baby at home," I say aloud.

"Y-you're threatening my child?" he says.

I ram my face into his. "No. I'm threatening you. Go home to your wife, to the blessing she was naïve enough to give you, and stop chasing women." I bite out my last few words. "If you ever pull this shit again, I'll yank out your spine and stab you through the skull with it."

I ease away from him, giving him enough space for a quick, if not, clumsy exit.

A satisfied smirk splays across my lips.

Celia gapes at me. "That was awful."

"Yeah," I agree. "What an asshole."

"I meant your behavior," she replies.

"What do mean?" I frown. "I didn't hit him or anything."

She throws out her hands. "Aric, you scared him to death."

I cross my arms, watching him disappear into the building. "You're welcome, baby."

She blinks back at me and then laughs, covering her face as she cracks up.

I've gone too long without seeing that lovely face. I pull her hands away carefully and kiss each one. She's warm, despite the cold.

The heat from her skin deepens the longer I hold her.

She smiles softly. "What are you doing here, Aric?"

I lose my grin. "I've come to save you. Celia. You're in danger..."

Chapter Six

"You're here to save me?" she repeats, evidently unimpressed.

I nod. "That's right."

She raises her eyebrows. "From Dr. Bantam?"

I scoff. "If so, you're welcome." I hook a thumb in the direction that moron took off. "He's probably busy changing his pants."

She laughs again, reaching for me. "Come on. Let's get you home."

I jog back to retrieve her small backpack. It's already coated with snow. "Home? To your place?"

"Of course," she says. "My sisters are going to lose their minds."

Her voice falls silent and her eyes glaze over.

My fingers link through hers, my touch stirring her awake. "What's wrong?" I ask.

"Nothing," she says. She glances around as if forgetting where she is. "This is my last of seven shifts in a row."

"Seven?" I allow her to lead me forward and away from the section of homes. "You work twelve-hour shifts, don't you?" I smile and nudge her playfully. "You did it, right? You accomplished your goals and became a nurse."

My praise is enough to flush Celia's frost-nipped cheeks. "I did. It was so much harder than I expected."

As quick as her smile appears, it vanishes, that deadened expression threatening to return. "What is, sweetness?" I ask.

"I..." she waits, struggling to gather her thoughts. "I only usually work three shifts a week, but this is probably Ana Lisa's last Christmas with us. I need the money and the time off." She shrugs, but the lift in her shoulders is very slight. "Another nurse planned a skiing trip. I covered her shifts so she could go. In exchange, she's covering the holidays so I can be home with my family."

She looks ahead. "Come," she says. "I need to get home and we need to be fast."

She starts to take off in a sprint. I hold her in place. It's cold, she's tired, and she needs to be home with her sick foster mother, and her sisters. I understand, but there's more going on. Celia isn't just distracted. There's something wrong with her.

"Is someone hurting you?" I ask. "Another doctor or co-worker?"

"No." She presses her lips. "Look, I'm aware what they say about me."

"They?" I ask.

"The hospital staff. They comment about my body and looks when they think I can't hear them. But when they see me and sense my tigress, they stop acknowledging me altogether." Her voice drops. "They back away from the scary beast tasked with protecting me."

I have an inner wolf. He's a part of me, but I'm the one in charge. Celia has a golden tigress lingering inside her soul. Celia can't always control her. Unlike my wolf, her tigress is almost a separate entity and is ferocious when it comes to protecting Celia.

The big cat peeks through just enough to warn others away. Everyone, except that doctor who was smart enough to get through school, but too arrogant to listen to his instincts.

Celia is right about others keeping their distance from her. Her tigress is crazy protective, and the reason Celia can't make friends. Still, something else is wrong, and likely the reason Mimi sent me.

"Is there anything else?" I press. "Something that's scaring you?"

She pauses to consider me. Again, it's like her thoughts travel elsewhere. But then it's as if she understands what she should say, instead of what actually is.

"Ana Lisa is really sick," Celia admits. "As the sole provider, I can't afford a car right now and run to and from work." She points in the direction of the nearby neighborhoods. "This way home is longer, but the jog helps my tigress settle." She shakes her head when I make a beeline toward the first development and guides me in the opposite direction. "We have to take the shorter way through Somerville. It's not ideal. The alpha bear who runs the local pack has made it clear I'm not welcome on his turf." This time when she shrugs, it's obvious. "I've abided by his wishes to avoid a throwdown. But tonight, is different. I need to get home to my family."

She starts forward again in that odd manner she's been behaving. I pull her in for a kiss to help her settle, and maybe me settle too. The contact is tender but brief. Still, it doesn't lessen the passion or the intent behind it.

The chemistry between us is enough to snap her out of the fog she's in. I reason she's just worried about her family. My wolf warns otherwise.

I push her wet hair away from her face. "We're going to make it safely back to your home," I tell her. "Not just cause we're fast, but because I'll take on an entire pack for you."

Her eyes blink back at me. "You will, won't you, wolf?" she asks quietly.

I return her soft smile, in a way of an answer and release her. She backs away from me, smiling once before whirling around and sprinting away. I catch up swiftly, keeping pace beside her.

It takes a block or so to find the right rhythm. Her stride is strong, but my legs are a lot longer than hers. She has to move faster to remain beside me, not that she seems to mind. If anything, she appears to enjoy the release of energy.

I'm not one to talk while I run. It's not that I can't do it, it's more like me and my wolf are too wrapped up in the freedom of it to allow words to interrupt the moment. With Celia here, I want to talk and know everything she's experienced in our time apart.

I open my mouth at the same time she does. We laugh. "You first," I tell her, not wanting to admit how much I love hearing her voice.

"You said you're here to protect me," Celia says. "Do you think it's from Odin, the werebear?"

"No," I say, reasoning through her thoughts. "You avoid his territory, right?" She nods. "We're only cutting through his turf because you need to get home and I've delayed your return."

"That's right," she agrees.

"I wasn't sent to put you in danger. I was sent to save you from it. Whatever I'm here for is evil. Alphas trying to keep other supernaturals from their turf shouldn't equate on such a catastrophic level."

"Then what else can it be?" she asks. Again, her voice fades.

I eye her closely. "I'm not sure," I admit. "Mimi sent me. She drew ley lines, fussing over time continuums and working her spell with runes. She stressed how darkness surrounds you."

"That's nothing new," Celia reminds me quietly.

No. It's not. There's something about Celia and her family that makes things that go bump in the night want to take her out. The reminder toughens my voice. "I realize that, Love. Mimi sent me to protect you, stressing that your life was in peril."

Celia's speed slows briefly. "Are you okay?" she asks. "I'm sorry. I'm trying to wrap my head around all this." She laughs without meaning it. "I can't get past that Mimi is alive, let alone understand why she sent you to me." She smiles in that same sad way. "But I won't complain."

"I won't either," I agree. No matter how much Mimi makes my wolf want to tear his fur out, the hag did reunite me and Celia.

Streetlamps, with bulb covers yellowed with time, light most of our way. As fast as we're going, it's not fast enough to alert the speeding cars we pass of our supernatural footprint. Most of the intersections we reach permit us through without breaking our stride, but as the suburban terrain slips away and we reach smaller and more congested sections, I know the town's center isn't much farther.

"How old are you, Aric?"

It should sound like a strange question, except that it's not. In real time, I'm two years older than Celia. The last time we met we were the same age, but only because the space time continuum was altered by a spell meant to spare her life.

"I'm eighteen." I fight the cold snap that strikes my bare arms. "It's almost spring back home."

Celia manages a few slow breaths, their visibility barely perceptible in the snow. "I'm nineteen. Christmas is in two days."

"I picked up on that," I say. The tension accelerates in the quiet that follows. Our time together is brief, and we both know it.

She wants to say more. I do, too. But the misery between us is as palpable as the snow slapping against our faces. It keeps us silent. As does the knowledge of our inevitable goodbye.

We pass several more blocks before she speaks again.

"Why is this happening?" she asks.

"I don't know," I admit. It's all I can say, the words of comfort I seek are too far from my reach.

"It's cruel that we have to keep meeting like this." She swallows hard. "Is not remembering supposed to be some show of mercy?"

"Mimi has no mercy to give," I admit, bothered by how much I mean it. I'm out of my mind to see Celia again, but like she says, it's cruel.

The light at the intersection changes, forcing us to stop. I take her by surprise by lifting her in my arms and kissing her. It's not as long as I want, and it's not all I want to do, but I'll take any moment I can share with Celia.

My shirt is soaked through, and if I wasn't running as fast as I was, I'd freeze. Celia doesn't care, leaning into me even as I lift my mouth from hers.

"I don't know why I'm here," I murmur against her lips. "All I know is that I'm here for you and that's good enough for me."

She smiles, appearing reluctant to move when the light changes. "More later, okay?" she glances up ahead. "The storm isn't letting up and we have to keep moving."

It's only because I know she's right that I let her go.

We reach the downtown quickly. Instead of cutting through the back lots and alleyways, Celia takes me down the main street. Smart. Enough humans linger and some shops remain open. The activity will make the local pack think twice about starting trouble.

I extend out my senses to be sure. Buildings erected sometime during the 1800s line either side of the street while more modern buildings stretch out along the side streets.

It's two worlds spread out in a small area. Somehow it works. Where typewriter repair shops and small grocery stores once stood, trendy clothing stores and restaurants now lure in current shoppers, promising a good sale or a delicious meal.

Jersey is not my idea of a good time. It's also not what I expected. Not this side of it, anyway. Everything that screams Christmas: twinkling lights, garland, and mistletoe dangle and adorn every post and window along this small piece of America. Not in a bad way. It's nice. Pretty. There aren't any cheap plastic decorations, overinflated snowmen, or reindeer waving hello with their hooves. There's just cheer, I guess. The kind I've forgotten since Dad died.

I shouldn't sense that cheer now, not with Celia in danger and what I might have to face. But with her presence this close, things *are* better. We're unstoppable, she and I. As lame as it sounds, I can take on anything with her by my side. Anything.

Until she's gone.

Celia increases her speed, racing us past large open alleys blocked off from cars. They must have concerts here in the summer, show movies, and have performances. Just like they do back home. It's perfect, given all the places to eat. I wish I could take Celia to dinner here, on a real date. I wish I could celebrate Christmas with her, spoil her rotten with gifts, and kiss her under the mistletoe. Except her well-being is the priority and, knowing Mimi, I won't have the luxury of more than a few days.

Mimi didn't come out and say it, but knowing her, the minute my mission is complete, she'll yank me far from Celia and drop me in a pile of manure.

My wolf perks up as the energy shifts, pulling me back into the moment. Almost at once, everything starts to shut down. The few and daring last minute shoppers huddle into their scarves and rush to their cars. Unlike us, they slide here and there, almost falling in their haste to reach shelter.

Lights flicker off as shop owners close down for the night. A couple disappears into the rear of a jewelry store and out the backdoor.

"I was hoping to hide in the open," Celia says, quietly. "Too late for that, now."

She slows her pace to a jog. We're still in hurry, but like me, she knows we're being watched.

I see him half a second before Celia. A man with dark skin and a beard eyes us from an apartment window above a trattoria. He's muscular and tall, dwarfing the woman rocking the small baby on her hip. He's one of the bears. I can tell by his dense build and the way he carries himself.

He says something to the woman, his attention, never leaving us. She nods and hurries off. I don't hear his snarl, but I catch it in the way he glares.

Bring it on, bitch. You don't scare me.

"We can make a run for it," Celia suggests.

"No," I say, though I recognize she's not thrilled with her own suggestion. "It will only make us look bad."

She crinkles her nose. "And stepping on their turf doesn't?" she asks.

Man, she's cute. "The guilty tend to run," I say. "I don't want the alpha to think we came here to cause trouble and hauled ass to avoid getting caught." I shrug. "He knows we're here. Might as well meet him, one leader to another."

"Do you think it will work?"

"Maybe. Maybe not. What I do know is if we run, we'll be perceived as threats. The bear will be in his right to hunt us outside his jurisdiction and even into to your home." I frown when something occurs to me. "How do you know him anyway?"

"I don't really know him." Celia makes a face. "I wandered into his territory before I knew there was territory to wander into. There aren't many packs in this state. Mostly because there's not a lot of space for *weres* to run, unlike Upstate New York and the rural parts of Pennsylvania."

"All right," I say. "So, he approached you directly?"

"Not exactly. It's more like he picked a fight with me."

"What?" Okay, now I'm pissed. "He can't just challenge you for wandering onto his turf."

"It's not like that. One of his mountain lions slapped my butt—"

Celia's eyes widen when she gets a good look at my face.

"*What?*" I ask, my voice more beast than man.

"Ah, it was more like a stroke." She cuts herself off, knowing she's digging this *were* a bigger grave. "Aric, it's all right."

"How the hell is someone touching you without your consent all right?" I demand.

"It's not," Celia says. "Which is why I ripped his arm off and smacked him across the face with it."

"You..." I choke back a laugh. For all she's sweet, my rose has some serious thorns.

She nibbles on her bottom lip. "I wasn't quite out of Somerville when Odin got word I'd assaulted a member of his pack. He and a few of his *weres* approached me as I reached the outskirts. He made it clear I wasn't welcome anywhere near his pack. I think he realized I could kill one of his own. Although he was angry, he didn't retaliate since his packmate acted first."

It's what he claimed. Given the severity of her response, and the fact that she's a non-*were*, I think Odin was bothered a *were* under his watch had disrespected a female. If I'm right, that's a good thing. It makes him honorable. I wouldn't bet on it, but it's something to consider.

"All right," I say. I'm still enraged at how she was treated, but I have to remain in the here and now. "It's only a matter of time before Odin shows. Let me do the talking. Don't respond with violence unless we have to."

It's crazy that this is what I'm telling her. Responding with violence is my M.O.

Celia nods. "Okay. Let's just...Let's just make it quick. My family is probably worried."

I glance behind us, making sure we're not being followed. "Maybe you should call them, let them know you're all right."

Celia's eyes glaze over, her voice ghostly. "The phones don't work anymore," she says. "Nothing is going as it should. Emme and Shayna barely passed this semester, Taran, too. They're crying all the time. They barely leave their room."

I stop dead. "What is happening to your family?"

I clasp her shoulders when she doesn't respond. She jolts at my contact, lifting her hand to push me away before she realizes what she's doing. "What?"

"Aw, hell," I mutter, realizing what's happening. "Celia. The evil I'm supposed to stop has invaded your house. It's why everything's going wrong in your home."

Her breathing quickens as if she's run all day instead of a few miles. Again, her irises glaze over. "It's her," she rasps. "She brought them and won't let them leave."

Chapter Seven

"Who is she?" I ask. I give her a small shake. "Celia, tell me who's in your home."

Celia rams her eyes closed as if pained, shaking her head slowly. When she opens her eyes, she appears confused. "What... what just happened?"

I don't mention her house or what's there. Every time she thinks of her family or her home, she goes somewhere she shouldn't.

"Don't worry," I say. I can't keep the fury from my tone even as I tuck her against me. "I'm going to fix it. I promise."

I jerk my attention forward, having second thoughts about making a run for it. If evil indeed shrouds Celia's home, the pack here, provided they honor the pledge we make to guard the earth, are obliged to help us expunge the darkness. But if they're somehow involved or ill-fit to fight it....

I mutter a curse. This pack is new according to Celia. For all I know they've gone rogue. I can't trust them. Not yet.

The snowfall lessens in severity. It's our only saving grace. It's not much. It's just enough to permit me to see farther ahead.

As much as my wolf fights it, I release Celia so she can walk beside me instead of keeping her pressed to my side. It's hard to do. I want to shield her and take the brunt of what follows. Except if we're jumped, both of my hands need to come out swinging.

We pass by a café with all its lights out. I nudge Celia subtly and cut my gaze toward the glass front door. The dark outline of a female slinks back and out of sight. This for sure is a new pack. The *weres* I was raised with hide much better than this. We can rush and kill an opponent before he realizes we're even there. This female all but blasted a horn to announce her presence.

The next set of *weres* don't care about hiding. They should if they're looking to overtake us. Two males, wolves from what I can tell, and a female lynx step out from the shadows in human form and trail us.

The lynx makes a hissing sound. Celia glances over her shoulder to meet her square in the eye. I smirk at the way the wolves frown, clearly put off by Celia's lack of fear.

That's right, boys. My pussy can beat yours in a fight.

Celia gasps, then covers her face, giggling. "*Aric.*"

I lose my game face and laugh right along with her. "Sorry. Did I say that out loud?"

Even through this damn snow I catch her blush.

I also catch what the wolves behind me have to say.

"She called him Aric," one wolf says.

"So what?" the lynx asks.

The wolves ignore her, speaking amongst themselves. "It can't be him. Not here, not with her."

My hands ball into fists. They better not mean it like I think they did.

I'm known worldwide for my unique ability to *change* into my beast at a freakishly and unheard of age. I'm also known for my skill and strength. I should be used to it. Yet somehow, it doesn't seem right for these fools to know me.

"Oh, him," the lynx says, her tone enticed. "That hot piece of *were* wouldn't be here. And like Max says, definitely not with her when I'm around."

This time, when Celia glances over her shoulder, her tigress eyes meet the lynx's and her claws protrude from her fingertips.

I smooth an arm around Celia's shoulder for two reasons: One, she has nothing to worry about. Two, these clowns need to respect that yes, she's with me and no one will ever be what Celia is to me.

We're almost to the end of the street when the aroma of splitting pines and rushing river water poke through the dimness.

Odin materializes through the thick veil of snow. The bear we spotted at the window stands on his right. A shorter, stockier male waits at his left, his hands clasped in front of them. Like both *weres* on either side of him, Odin is beefy in build.

A tight, slightly wet shirt stretches across his torso and gray sweatpants cover his legs. Every member of his pack is dressed in clothing that's easy to tear through when they *change* into their beasts.

My jeans are practically frozen to my legs and my shirt is worse off. If I handle this diplomatically, the way my father would, I may not have to *change* at all. There might not even be a fight. Except I don't like the contempt being thrown Celia's way. They know she's not *were* and view her as far beneath them. This is no way to appeal to my diplomatic side.

Odin crosses his arms, assuming a position of authority. I do the same, keeping my arms loose and slightly lower, ready to strike if necessary.

"I told you not to come here," Odin says as a way of an introduction. "Not only did you disobey me, you brought a friend." He jerks his head in my direction. "Didja think I'll let it slide cuz he's a wolf?"

"No," Celia replies. Her tone is stiff, making it clear she's not afraid and owes him nothing. "I'm not a child to reprimand, or your subordinate to order as you see fit."

"This is *my* territory," Odin bites back all but roaring at her. He finds Celia's defiance insulting and is asserting his dominance. In his beast form, he'd already be snapping his jowls.

He plans to make an example out of her. *Yeah, go ahead and try.*

"*Who the fuck are you?*" Odin growls.

I'll give him this. He realizes I'm the bigger threat. "Aric Connor," I answer, my tone clipped.

As an alpha meeting another, etiquette demands I introduce myself as the son of Aidan and Eliza Connor and give him my rank. I don't bother with formalities. They're looking to fight, not talk.

The smaller bear edges forward, Celia warns him with a hiss. "You're a liar," he tells me. "Ain't no way you're him."

I frown, not because of what he says, but of what I catch in his aroma.

Odin sucks his teeth. "Aric Connor? You're that young alpha bigshot running half the packs across Colorado? Bitch, you better pretend to be someone else," he warns.

Celia glances at me. Running the packs of Colorado? That's news to her and me.

I'm never caught off guard. I am at this news.

The barrel of a gun presses into the base of my skull and the sour scent of cursed gold bullets pierce my nose.

I raise my hands. "We're doing it this way?" I spit through my teeth.

Odin prowls toward me, whispering low into my ear. "We're doing it anyway I want to."

The move I make is too fast for Odin to track. Having rehearsed it a thousand times since childhood, it's more like breathing than anything I purposefully do.

I bend my knees, pivoting down and round the wolf with the gun. His neck snaps as my arm locks around it and I ram my knee into his lower back.

He's not dead. It takes more than a broken neck to kill us. But he knows he's in trouble.

In his panic, he starts firing. I let him, guiding his wrist and using him as a shield when *weres* leap from rooftops and scramble out from alleys. Nineteen total, including the six I force my prey to shoot.

I fling the *were's* flaccid form into the mountain lions gunning for me. I use the momentum to add more force to the spinning kick I nail a wolf with. Between the shots fired and how fast I take out the next two *weres* who jump me, the others fall back, circling me with caution.

A young wolf clutches his side, crying from poison the cursed gold bullet is pumping into his system. It burns. We're taught how to push through the pain in school, but these *weres* weren't taught anything, from what I see.

I scan my surroundings, keeping them in my sights as I search for Celia.

Celia?

"Get away from him or he dies," she snaps.

If it weren't for the danger we're in, I'd laugh or at least smirk when I catch sight of her. But given the numbers on their side, all I want to do is mow through the lot of them and reach her.

Celia's back is pressed against the brick exterior of a bakery. She has Odin in a choke hold and her legs wrapped around his waist. He writhes beneath her. He's stronger and it won't be long before he breaks free. Still, she made her point: the only reason he's still alive is because she's allowed it.

She protrudes her nails slowly, allowing them to slice into Odin's scalp and draw blood. "I said, 'Let him go,'" she hisses.

Gasps and growls erupt in my perimeter. This pack can't manage something as minor as a poker face.

It takes all my will not to yank him from Celia and kill him myself—not just for threatening us, but for running such a pathetic pack.

My steps are deliberate, my resolve crumbling when I catch the bruise across Celia's face and the way she favors her left side. She didn't take down the alpha unscathed. As someone who heals only slightly faster than a human, he could have killed her if he caught her just right.

I swallow hard. Revenge has become my bedmate and my wolf demands we demonstrate how well we wield it. But I'm not here to avenge my father or take out my assigned target. I'm here to stop the evil infecting Celia's home. That won't happen if I give every last *were* in the region cause to come after us.

"Let him go, sweetness," I say.

My term of endearment sends another wave of discord across the pack.

Celia locks eyes with me, her limbs shaking with how hard she's fighting to hold Odin. "You sure?" she asks, her voice trembling.

At my nod she releases him, rolling forward and into a standing position before Odin finishes rising.

Celia angles herself so she can watch me and the pack, her chest rising and falling from the rush of adrenaline that kept her alive.

Odin and I are breathing just as fast, and it's not due to the rush of battle. Celia humiliated him in front of his pack. Me, I'm livid that he could have hurt her much worse.

Odin tries to turn it around to save face. "You're him then, the alpha of Colorado?" He huffs. "The youngest Leader of our kind and the one set to supervise that new den they're building in Tahoe?"

"I am Aric Connor," I reply. "Son of Aidan and Eliza Connor, and you have seriously wronged us."

He, like all *weres,* should be able to sniff a lie. Except as green as most of them are, they're either untrained to do it or struggling because of moisture in the air. In case they can distinguish what's true and what isn't, I have to choose my words carefully. Except, it's not that easy.

I don't know what's happening during this time period. I have no idea why Martin would entrust me with half the packs in Colorado. And a Den in Tahoe? As much as I mocked this pack's game face, mine is dwindling fast.

Celia's presence beside me reminds me I need to stay in the moment and keep us alive.

"I didn't know who you were," he says. It's not exactly an apology. Like I thought, he's trying to keep face. "I also didn't know who she was to you."

"Now you do," I say. I ease away, taking that bit of leverage he hands me to address the pack.

The *were* whose neck I snapped is still recovering, two of his packmates including the lynx keep him still so his spine can properly realign.

"You allow your pack to chamber guns with cursed gold bullets?" I ask Odin. "It only kills *weres* and vamps. As for humans..." I shrug. "A bullet to the body is all the same. No gold needed." I meet his face, my jaw tightening. "Who exactly are you after?"

The fall of snow seizes enough for the quarter moon to poke through the dwindling clouds.

"My pack is small, vulnerable. I do what it takes to keep them safe," Odin replies. He spits at the ground. "Treaty or not, you can't trust dem bloodsuckers around here."

I reach for Celia's hand and draw her close to me. These *weres* know better than to attack us now, but my wolf and I need her close.

This pack isn't supposed to remember what happened once I leave. They'll have no memory of me or how we brought them down. But maybe they'll remember just enough to give her space when I'm gone.

"If there's a vampire clan, you go through the proper channels. You don't weaponize as you see fit." My attention stops on each *were*, fixating on the bear who made the first move. "Where did you find these *weres*? They're rash and careless."

"They're *learning*," Odin states. He doesn't appreciate the insult. To his credit, there's honesty behind each word. "Most were *lones*, Alpha. Unable to be controlled by their human mamas or cast out by their *were* daddies. Jersey doesn't have a lot of *weres* and there ain't no *pures* throwing money at me to help them."

"I see," I say.

In those mere words I make it clear I understand beyond what he admits. He stiffens. He knows where I'm headed and doesn't like it. Tough. I tell him anyway. "You're one of those cast out yourself, aren't you?" His silence is response enough. "Your dedication to helping, while admirable, isn't enough." I stand off with him and lay it all out there. "Your pack needs more than you can offer."

Odin straightens to his full height. He doesn't like the public shaming, mostly because it's true.

I keep talking. He needs to understand that I mean to help, not damage his pack further. "Call the upstate New York alpha tonight. His name is Altman Moor. Don't mention me," I add quickly. "Come forward as the leader your *weres* need. Altman is a pureblood, capable of giving you the money and training you need. He's a good Leader. One of the best. He may even help you build your own Den."

"I'm no *pure*," Odin says. "He won't appreciate what all I made here."

In other words, I went against our ways and fear the repercussions.

He's right to fear Altman's wrath. Except an alpha isn't given an area as large as upstate New York if he can't rule it justly. Our ways are strict, disciplined, and at times vicious. But there is forgiveness for those who deserve it. If I'm right, Odin deserves leniency and assistance to make this pack all that he envisions.

"If you take responsibility for the lack of order and the mess you helped create, Altman and the Leaders will respect you for it," I explain. "There's a good chance you'll be forgiven."

"And there's a good chance they'll cut my head off," Odin rumbles. He rams his finger in my direction. He remains a few feet away. It's the only reason I don't respond with violence.

"I've led them the best way I know how," he hollers. "I gave them shelter, food, and a pack. Not like those mother fuckers who threw them out on the street." He sucks his teeth. "You talkin' about lack of order? Nothing goes down within a hundred-mile radius without me knowing about it. Nothing."

It's the opening I was waiting for. "Does that mean you're aware of the drugs your packmate is selling to humans?"

Odin's frown is genuine. He didn't know. I figured. Drug Lords don't care how females are treated. Odin did. It's why it bothered him when his *were* touched Celia without her permission.

My attention returns to the smaller bear who initially stood at Odin's side. Odin follows my focus. Damn. For this *were* to stand by Odin as he did, Odin must trust him. This will hurt him, and the *were* will pay with blood.

I can't stop what will follow, even if I wanted to. These are our ways and what's kept us honorable.

"You're Roz, aren't you?" I ask.

Roz's face slacks, but he quickly recovers. "You don't know me," he says, his self-righteous attitude firmly in place.

The mountain lioness beside him smacks his shoulder. "Show respect," she warns. "He's *that* alpha."

Roz puffs out his chest, too stupid and arrogant to know his place.

"I don't know you," I agree. "What I know is you supply addicts. Is this your contribution to the pack?"

It's Odin who answers. "He has a job at the factory. I got it for him." It's what he says, but he's listening and doesn't like what he hears.

I squeeze Celia's hand when her gaze darts between me and Roz. She doesn't know how I know what I do. I only arrived a short while ago. She's worried my plan will backfire. I'm worried, too—about her and what's waiting for us at her house.

Except lies need to surface if this pack is ever to survive.

I square my shoulders speaking as one alpha to another. "A human approached me tonight. He smelled of heroin and withdraw. He told me, 'My boy Roz will meet you on the corner of East Main and Mechanic.' Roz here reeks of this man and his addiction."

"He's crazy, Odin," Roz tells him.

"Shut up," Odin growls.

All the anger Odin met me with is now directed at Roz. Odin hears my truth as loudly as he hears Roz failure to deny it. Why would Roz lie anyway? It wouldn't help him. Weather be damned. His alpha can smell through the deception.

"There's no good reason a human would meet a *were* on a night like this," Odin bites out. "No good reason at all."

The *weres* surrounding Roz back away from him. Even those shot up with gold hold tight to their wounds and scramble away.

"Odin," Roz pleads, tears sliding down his cheeks. He knows what will happen. Just like he knows it's too late to stop it.

Odin addresses me. "My apologies for this night. Go in peace, Alpha."

His switch from urban to formal demonstrates his dedication to our kind. Yeah, he'll do right by his pack.

To Celia he nods. It's out of respect for me and respect for her strength. It may be enough to aid her long after I'm gone.

I press my hand against the small of her back and lead her out to the street. We round the corner as the crunch of bone precedes the last breath Roz will take.

Chapter Eight

The moment we're clear, Celia takes off running. I give chase, surprised she's not easy to catch. Injuries be damned, she doesn't let anything slow her down.

Celia stops short just before a stretch of highway. She bends forward, pressing her hands against her knees. "He killed him, didn't he?" she asks.

She's not really asking. The aroma of death is pungent and sharp, even from here. Celia can't sniff a lie. Yet the scent of death is something I wish I could spare her from.

Celia is breathing hard and it's not from the run. She isn't like my kind. Her conscience would also never allow her to be.

"He did," I say. I rub her back, wishing I could take her far away from everything that scares her.

Celia needs someone to take care of her, and that someone can only be me. I'm as certain of it as the magic that surrounds her.

She rights herself. "Will Odin kill more of his pack because of us?"

As *weres,* our beasts protect us spiritually as well as physically. They offer us comfort during our harshest trials, and give us strength when we're too weak to function. It's the only reason me and Mom are still alive.

Celia doesn't have that comfort. While her tigress can protect her from physical dangers, Celia's heart is all human. This world is brutal on someone with her love.

"Odin will do what he must to ensure his pack succeeds," I answer truthfully.

Celia looks down the white-coated highway, barren save for the few cars cautiously moving forward. Guilt tightens her voice. I don't have to know her like I do to hear it. "I take it that's a yes?"

"We're Guardians of the Earth." I don't intend to sound so callous when she'd benefit from kindness, and I'm uncertain why I don't use more care. "We're here to protect the world from evil, not advance the demise of man by supporting addiction."

She glances up at me. "Your duties are admirable. But your justice is as ferocious as your beasts."

"What do you expect?" I ask. "We are what we are."

I'm being a prick. My posture alone would send lesser *weres* bolting. Celia doesn't demonstrate the fear another preternatural would. She glides her fingertips down my arm, a gesture meant to ease my anger and comfort me.

My bones tense, threatening to crack. Even at my harshest, Celia breaks me down to rubble. She tilts her head, scrutinizing me closely. "What is it?"

I jerk my chin ahead, rebuffing the gentleness she offers. "This the way back to your place?" I ask.

"Yes," she answers carefully.

"Then we should go, shouldn't we?" Man, I hate this stone-cold demeanor I assume. Against my enemies it serves me well. Around her it's wrong. She deserves better.

"We should," she agrees quietly. "Try to keep up.

Charged by what awaits, or what she sees in me, Celia leaps over the mound separating us from the highway and jets away. Beneath the snow's cushioned layer is a frozen sheet of ice. Celia, more human than beast, should skid at least once or twice. She doesn't. Her tigress keeping her pace and balance and offering the protection she'll need when I'm gone.

To the lowly drivers still in drudges and trying to reach home we're mere blurs. The distance and darkness are enough to keep us camouflaged.

Celia continues to favor her side. It's barely perceptible as she pushes through the pain. That doesn't mean I'm not worried.

It's not until we cross the highway and disappear into a small section of trees that I attempt to ask her if she's all right. She beats me to anything I could possibly say.

She whirls on me, her movements graceful and unusually fast. "Aric, as an alpha who oversees the packs in Colorado, will you be charged with making decisions like Odin?"

"If I'm really in charge, the alphas in the smaller packs will lead according to our laws and see to those who break them. Alphas who oversee other packs address problems that are too much for their subordinates to handle alone."

"*If* you're really in charge?" Celia asks.

I shrug. "That's right."

"My present is your future," she says. "I realize you're still young in my reality, probably twenty-two, but you appear a little too surprised to learn you've assumed such a role."

"That's because I am," I tell her flatly.

"Why?" she questions. "Surely, your father trained and guided you to take on such a respected position?"

"Sure," I say.

Celia crosses her arms. Instead of meeting me with the anger I deserve, she appears worried. "Why are you acting this way?" she presses. Again, I shut my trap. "Given your familial legacy and the regard you're held in, does it seem like such an impossibility that you would oversee half the *weres* in Colorado?"

"Yeah, it does."

I don't move except for the harsh intakes of breath I take. This isn't the time to lash out or to take out the misery I've endured for the last two years on the closest tree.

She studies me closely. "Why?" she asks. "What exactly happened?"

What hasn't happened is more like it. And maybe what haven't I done? The pain I've inflicted, the nightmares I've awoken to, where do I begin? Hell, should I begin at all?

My focus wanders around the area of snow and dense brush we linger in. Just down a glen littered with garbage, a small herd of deer gathers beneath the trees. They take off when they spot us, their instincts to live warning them to run.

They're adult and good-sized deer. Odd, considering there's no real place for them to grow and thrive. This is no forest. Not like home. Not like the wilderness generations of my family grew up in.

The dirty scent of leftover exhaust creeps through the line of trees and the nearest cross-section remains only a few yards ahead. This isn't a real place for deer or *weres* to roam. Is it a wonder the local pack is so screwed up and removed from what it truly means to be a *were*?

I was too young to remember my first venture across the mountain I was raised on, just a wolf pup two months of age. My beast, though, remembers it well. Dad led, his huge wolf form paving the way through the forest floor swathed with stone and bark.

I followed behind as fast as my paws could carry me, stumbling through the thicket and tripping over anything I couldn't plow through. I raced after Dad, certain I could match his speed and run beside him. I wasn't afraid. Not with my father ahead, his tongue lolling with humor as I clumsily followed.

"Aric?"

"Not now, okay?" I say.

I can't look at Celia right now. Someone as beautiful as she doesn't belong amidst a wolf as bitter as me. The wickedness I never thought myself capable of saturates the air as viciously as the cold. I can feel it. I don't want her to feel it, too.

With more care than strength, she intertwines her fingers through mine and sets my hands between her breasts. Her heart beats against my knuckles and her aroma of water misting over stones pushes away the hate.

I take in the warmth each sweet touch of her skin awakens, drinking it in despite that I still can't meet her gaze. I know what's coming, and with Celia beside me, my truth stings so much more. I can't shield myself from my torment. Celia takes the rage I armed myself with and breaks it off in pieces. I'm no match against her.

"Aric," she says quietly. "Did something happen to your Dad?"

My jaw clenches tight, the muscles alongside them stiff and unyielding.

"My love, please tell me what happened?"

Her love. Yeah, sure. Until she knows the monster I've become.

"He's dead, all right?" I huff. "And in my time, my mother's just about ready to join him."

Celia gathers her thin arms around me, her voice breaking. "Oh, Aric, I'm so sorry."

It's all she says and it's enough. She doesn't need to tell me shit like, buck up, your people are counting on you, or remind me of the big shoes I now must fill, or that my father doesn't need my sorrow, the world needs my strength. "Your destiny awaits. Show them what you're made of, boy." That's the kind of idiocies my kind threw at me. There were expectations of me to just snap out of it and move on—that my unique *change* occurred for a reason, and it was time to fulfill my destiny.

Bastards. All of them. All the alphas who worried what would happen without the great Aidan Connor to guide them expected me to just swoop in and take his place. Every last one demanded I demonstrate leadership and knowledge beyond my years. Even my friends who constantly reminded me how awesome my father was, stood back waiting for me to become something no one could ever be ready to become.

I was only fifteen, damn it.

Yet no one would allow me to grieve for the hero and the man I called Dad.

Celia does. She weeps against my chest, joining me in the grief I was for so long denied.

I curse and hold her close. I curse some more and hold her tighter. I don't mean for those tears to escape like they do. Except this little thing in my arms is all it takes, her heart and love my undoing.

"I've messed up, Celia," I confess. "I've pulled some shit I never thought I'd be capable of."

The breeze picks up, dropping clumps of snow from the surrounding trees. Celia lifts her chin to better see me. She spares me from the "you could never do anything wrong" and the "everyone makes mistakes" bullshit.

She maintains her hold, something in my expression crinkling her brow with worry. "What have you done?"

The truth sharpens my voice. "You don't want to know," I reply.

Her voice splinters. "I want to know everything about you. All the good and the bad."

"I don't want...." I spit out another row of curses. Celia couldn't handle what happened to Roz. It was too barbaric for one *were* to do that to his packmate. "I don't want you to think less of me." I shake my head. "I couldn't handle it. Not from you."

"Aric, you know everything I've done." Her tears fade away, replaced by memories far worse than she deserves. "Those I murdered stain my soul with blood. No matter how much good I'll do in life, I'll never be absolved from my deeds."

"That wasn't murder," I tell her sternly. "*That* was justice."

"You call it justice," she says. "Maybe it was. That doesn't erase the fear of knowing how easily I can kill, and the ruthlessness I'm capable of."

I capture her mouth with mine. It's a slow kiss despite our rush, as loving and perfect as the woman I share it with. "Your humanity far surpasses your savagery, and your compassion vanquishes the cruelty you think you inflicted." I kiss her again. "Those you hunted, preyed on innocents and wreaked enough harm for a thousand lifetimes. They didn't deserve your mercy, just as you didn't deserve their violence."

She smiles despite the tears that sparkle in the moonlight. "You know my past so well, and still you stand by me."

I frown. "I love you. I'll always stand by you."

There're those tears again despite her delicate smile. "And I'll love and stand by you, no matter what."

Knowing her heart as well as I do, I shouldn't believe her. Not with what I must now share. Yet, I begin from the beginning even though my wolf warns against it. He's afraid to lose her, too. But hiding things from her is another form of lying. Lies between me and Celia are sins my beast and I won't allow.

"I avenged my father," I say. "I tracked the witch responsible for his death and made her pay."

Celia's eyes widen. "If she killed your father, she was strong enough to kill you."

"You're right," I agree. "And she almost did."

Celia's fear is as palpable as if I stood before the witch like I did then. It sounds crazy. I mean, I made it after all. But I guess that's what love is. Fearing for someone just because of what could happen.

"It started there, and it should have ended there. But it's like once I drew first blood, I couldn't stop." I try to shrug it off, but it's a half-assessed attempt at best.

"You liked the taste of it?"

Of killing, she means. "I did," I confess.

"My tigress did, too," she admits. "It's one of the reasons I couldn't stop." She glances down, her shame replacing her fear. "I couldn't stop her from hunting."

Even when it became too much for her human half.

"That's where we're different," I carefully explain. "I didn't want to stop and neither did my wolf. I went after anything and everything linked to the witch—*weres* who had protected her, men who had supplied her with sacrifices, even women who expanded the witch's reign by enticing males to join her."

"Why would so many collaborate with someone so heartless?" Celia asks when I quiet.

"Money, protection, and power," I answer. I hold her closer, trying to shield her from the cold and truth. "It's a poor nation. These people tire of going hungry and living in fear. It's easy for them to turn their backs on what's right when they can have so much more."

"I could never do that," Celia says. "I've been poor, I've gone hungry. But I could never help her destroy so many lives."

"I told myself the same thing," I admit. "It's what drove me to kill and what kept me going."

Celia rises on her toes to press a kiss against my cheek. It's only because I'm curled around her that she even reaches me. "I don't understand," she says. "From what you say, these beings are those you're supposed to protect innocents from."

"They are," I agree slowly.

Her misery breaks free. "Then why does your soul feel so broken?"

Damn if she doesn't nail it. The truth spills out before I can stop it. I bite out each word, telling Celia everything I've kept to myself. "I didn't do this for the world. I did it for me. I enjoyed the hunt—finding my prey cowering in shadows, fighting to the death when there was hardly any fight in me. I shed all that blood for me." Her eyes widen but her reaction only forces me to keep going. "I didn't just kill them. I hurt them. I inflicted as much pain as I could in the moments before they died. I imposed my dominance and forced my strength down their throats until they choked on it."

Celia listens intently, barely doing more than blinking away the tears that form. "That's not what alphas are supposed to do. Not the kind of alpha my father raised me to be." I shudder except it's not from the cold. "With every kill, I became someone I didn't recognize. There was no mercy, Celia. There was no desire to bring them before trial. I numbed myself from all the violence —no, I *basked* in it. Each time I stopped my prey's heart from beating, I became alive, not the walking dead I had become. The more I massacred, the more I thrived."

My breaths are harsh. I wait, in the silence that follows for the hatchet to fall and for Celia to leave me.

"No," she says simply.

"*No?*" I ask. "Didn't you hear me? I was—hell, *I am*, out of control. I only lived when I killed."

"If that were true, you would have killed all the *weres* in Odin's pack." Her gaze implores me to listen even as I fight not to. "You told me cursed gold bullets are so lethal, they can explode a *were's* heart."

"They can," I agree.

She adjusts her hold around me, and for a moment all I feel is that warmth she permeates. "Then why didn't you aim for their hearts, Aric? You had control over that bear's wrist. You could have killed six with that gun and those who charged you. If you're this out-of-control psychopath, why did you spare the whole pack?"

Her reasoning strikes a blow, harder than anything I endured tonight.

"You're not a murderer, Aric. You don't live to torture." Her eyes pool with fresh tears despite her soothing smile. "You just want your daddy back."

"My..."

I look around, but there's nothing to face except the truth.

I never mourned.

Never.

Not like I should have.

No one would let me. Not my friends who shadowed me, waiting for me to become the hero Dad was. Not my mother, who is so consumed with her own pain she barely sees me. Not Martin. Not my packmates.

I had a role to assume, after all.

God help me. I never *allowed myself* to feel every bit of my father's passing.

But Celia allows me. She gives me the permission I was, for so long, denied.

Maybe that's all I ever needed.

So, I oblige. And she lets me.

Celia tucks herself into me, reminding me she's here and isn't going anywhere.

She holds me. After all I've done, she simply holds me.

CHAPTER NINE

It takes some time before we move again. The start of more snow and the late hour is motivation enough.

"Let's get to your house. I need to make sure you and your family are safe."

Celia nods. She remains on edge, over me and her family, too. But then it's like she goes into her own little world that I'm not a part of.

I grasp her hand, the contact pulling her back to me and away from whatever snags hold of her.

We cross the next few neighborhoods. These houses are new and built on top of each other, leaving what little flora remains to fight for its survival. It's not until we cross into an older neighborhood that properties stretch larger in size.

The homes are small and modest. Most are brick and well-cared for in their old age. A small few should be condemned. They're well-past saving, even though the scent of the humans struggling inside drift to float among the lingering snowflakes.

"Are we almost there?" I ask.

Celia nods. "It's the next block over, at the end of the street and close to a small field. We'll cut through the back and hopefully sneak up on whatever might be there."

"Sounds good."

We jog past the remains of another house. What's left of the roof is covered with tarps, and plastic bags line several broken windows. The brick exterior is cracked and crumbling. Still, two old cars are parked in the driveway, and the smell of canned chicken soup gusts through the small openings.

I motion with a jerk of my chin. "Is your house like this?" I ask.

I don't mean it to sound like an accusation, but that's exactly how it comes out. I don't want Celia to live like this. I could give her a better life if Mimi and the space time continuum would let me.

"Aric, these families never had much to start with, and now they have even less," she explains, keeping her voice soothing. "They're not bad people. They just struggle more than most in the area."

"I'm not judging them," I say, meaning it. "I'm trying to get a fix on what might be invading your home." It's true. But like I said, I don't want her life to be as hard.

I start to explain when she starts fading away again. I squeeze her hand, giving her enough of me to lure her back.

She shakes out of the spell she appears to be under. I'm hoping she's starting to recognize it so she may push it away before it overwhelms her. "Please explain what you mean," she tells me. "I'm trying hard to understand but the supernatural remains a mystery I can't quite solve."

She's right, and it worries me.

"Humans can be sensitive to dark power," I explain. "Some are more attuned to it. They're the ones you refer to as psychics. There are also those who aren't as aware of it, but still react to the negative energy." I watch her closely, making sure all of her remains with me. "Those who are ill become sicker. If they're depressed or anxious, it worsens. If they're especially vulnerable to it, it can incapacitate them."

"Enough so they can't work or study?" Celia asks.

"Yes," I reply.

"It explains a lot." She motions back to the tarped-roof house. "That family has been out of work for months and as I mentioned, my sisters are struggling in school. They're stressed all the time and can't focus on anything."

"Let's see what we can do to change that," I reply, suppressing my growls.

We pass another home where empty water bottles and rusty cans poke through the ice-covered driveway.

Celia eyes the house as we push past it, her nose wrinkling when the stench of rot mixes with the aroma of dung. "Aric, everyone appears to be struggling around here. Is it because of us? Is all of this a result of something we've done?"

"No," I say firmly. "This is something beyond you and your abilities. I'm not sure why you're being targeted, but this ends tonight. I won't allow you or anyone else to suffer any further."

The look she pegs me with is one I remember well. It speaks of her fervent determination, the one that squashes all fear until only courage remains.

"Ready?" I ask.

Her smile is small but all the affirmation I need. "I am now," she replies.

She jogs to the end of the street, sticking to the shadows. The field is wide, offering enough coverage against prying human eyes. We keep low, our steps silent over the fresh layer of powder that forms.

This field has weathered through storms and all the neighborhoods erected around it. It's lifted a middle-finger at the changes and the hustle and bustle of children barreling through it. Like the small sections of flora we encountered, it's managed to survive.

I don't know much about the area, just what I've seen. But this old field will overcome, even if the surroundings fall to rubble. Of this, I'm absolutely sure.

I scan the area closer as we near Celia's neighborhood. I had an entire mountain to play on as a child. The children in the surrounding developments have this field. This is a space where several rounds of hide and seek were played, as well as few impromptu kickball sessions. Teens come to park here. This is where they'll take their first drag or sip of alcohol, and maybe share a first kiss.

As much as my wolf feels disdain towards the lack of space to roam, I think he wouldn't mind it as much if we shared it with Celia.

We reach the edge of the clearing where a smaller and older neighborhood spreads out before us. Instead of brick, aluminum siding covers these homes. Small cement stoops make up the front porch, and curved dirt paths replaces concrete driveways.

This street was constructed for small families with just enough income to pay the bills and keep food on the table. All it needs is the right theme song to define the era it was created for.

The biggest indication that things are not quite how they should be is the lack of Christmas spirit. Unlike the downtown, mere miles from here, there's nothing to indicate that the holidays are well underway. There's only the quiet and dimness that comes when things have taken a turn toward the very wrong.

Celia crouches down. Like me, she's likely starved and in need of a warm bath. I'll see she gets what she needs. I'll always see to what she needs. Except it may not be tonight.

The wind shifts, pelting us with another layer of snow as her neighborhood darkens far beyond the normal veil of the night.

"Which is your house?" I ask.

"The green one, three houses down on the left."

I nod. "Okay."

We take off, cutting through the closest backyard. An old set of patio furniture sits beneath a giant oak, another layer of rust likely forming beneath the inches of new snow. Plastic pots, some empty, some housing long dead plants, trail along the rear patio. Like the plants, this yard is long forgotten.

I shadow Celia, hiding behind the trees that border the next yard.

A giant hole takes up most of this property. Roots from trees as old as time push through the sides. Someone had attempted to build a pool back here. They didn't know what they were doing, or gave up when the negative energy became too much. They finished the outline, but not much more.

We lurk to the edge, hiding behind a stack of cinderblock.

"This it?" I ask.

Celia presses her lips and nods, peering at her home as if she expects it to attack.

The other yards weren't cared for. Not by a long shot. Between the clutter and the abandoned projects, what could have been nice properties were abandoned and deemed unsalvageable. Celia's house, for all it's supposedly being cloaked by evil, isn't like the others.

The yard is clean. Several inches of snow cover what's likely a meticulously kept lawn. My guess is that Celia's charged with mowing it all summer long. Who else would? She's the strong one. There's a garden perched near the end, scrupulously maintained, and awaiting the first taste of spring.

Two small stone steps lead up to an enclosed porch, the windows thin and barely enough to keep out winter's wrath. Along the porch's concrete base, clay pots are stacked in neat rows.

The entire scene appears normal. *Too* normal.

As late as it is, there aren't any lights on in the house. There's no blast from a T.V., no inkling of movement. Someone should be up waiting on Celia, except the only thing that greets us is quiet.

I extend out my senses, searching for anything supernatural. I'm drawn to the sky above Celia's house. I expect to see something. But again, only quiet awaits.

Until that darkness that shouldn't belong stirs, creeping out of the house and stretching out toward us.

"Do you see anything?" Celia asks.

"No," I admit. "But I feel it. It's coming right at us."

"I sense it, too," she agrees. "I just can't understand why I never noticed it before."

"Dark entities don't simply manifest out of nowhere. Only real powerful ones have that ability. For something to infect your home like it has, my guess is that the attack was small and imperceptible at first. Too subtle to notice. As time has passed, it's become part of your house, building and feeding off you."

"Like a parasite," she realizes.

"Exactly," I say, wishing I could spare her from how bad it is. "You're the strongest in your family. It's why you're still working and able to leave the home."

I shake off the feel of something trying to ensnare me. This thing, spell, I'm guessing, is bold enough to attempt to latch on to me. Nice try, but neither me nor my beast will allow it.

"Did something just go after you?" Celia asks. "I felt it approach but then it was gone."

"As soon as I felt it, I shoved it away. I want you to do the same, okay? Imagine yourself pushing the darkness away as strongly as you would a physical being. Except instead of using your hands, use your magic, your spirit. Let it know you're the boss and it can't take you."

At first, Celia seems unsure. Her magic remains very foreign to her. She never wanted it, just as she never wanted to believe monsters were real.

Yet she's accepted the curse meant to kill her, and has doggy-paddled as best she could through the supernatural pool. Most would have keeled over and died. But Celia isn't most. She squares her shoulders and sets her small jaw, demonstrating the resolve I know and love.

I force myself back in the game, mulling through our best options. My wolf compels me forward. He wants to scour the perimeter, get a sense of what we're fighting, and make our way in.

Fine. Sounds like a plan.

I permit my wolf forward without allowing him all the way through. "It's time," I say in a low growl. "Stay here."

She clasps my arm. "Wait—*what*?"

I cock my head, unsure what the problem is. "Stay here while I kill whatever's invaded your house. As soon as I'm done, I'll come fetch you."

I do a double-take when my beloved glares at me, like *glares* as if ready to kill me.

"Fetch me? Really, Pa?" She smiles. It's not one of her prettier smiles. If I'm not mistaken, she's ready to bite. "Can I bake you a pie afterward? Maybe mend your socks by the fire? You know how I love to mend dem socks after a good fetchin'."

"You're not going with me," I tell her. "It's too dangerous for someone as fragile as you."

Why is she looking at me that way?

"I can see your prowess with the ladies is on point as always," she mutters.

"Celia, be reasonable," I tell her.

"Don't tell me to be reasonable. There's something evil in my house, eating away at my soul, and my family's, for months. I'm going with you, whether you like it or not. And don't you *ever* call me fragile again."

She jabs me in the chest with her finger for emphasis. The last creature who did that to me, I broke his finger off and made him eat it. With Celia, I just find myself smiling. She's seriously cute, even when she appears ready to punch my skull in.

I give her a quick kiss. "You're staying here," I order. "When I finish off the creature, I'll come for you and—"

It's then the delicate little darlin flips over the cinderblocks, lands in a forward roll and stalks toward the house all in one fluid move.

I tackle her and roll her away from the steps. Using my weight, I straddle her and pin her hands over her head. "I told you to stay put."

She blinks back at me, her tone matter-of-fact. "Get off me before I kill you."

Her attitude shouldn't turn me on, especially at a time like this. But it's like my wolf went from hating females and straight into heat the moment we saw Celia.

"No," I reply. "I don't think I will."

"Aric, good looks and charm won't help you now," she says.

I smirk. "You think I'm good looking and charming? Tell me more."

"Get off me or face the full wrath of my inner beast."

Her voice cuts off as warmth fills my face. It's not anything she says, it's just her. Her long wavy hair I want to drag my fingers through, her flawless olive skin I can't wait to taste, and those large green eyes that will always see the real me.

And that mouth? I'll only stop kissing it to kiss other parts.

"I don't want to fight with you," I manage. Nope. Fighting is not what I have in mind right now.

I don't need a mirror to realize how my gaze heats. We don't know what's waiting for us inside. But me on top of Celia like this stands everything at attention. *Everything*. I can't control myself around her. And I'll be damned if I want to.

Celia swallows hard, the heat from her blush pelting her body and tightening the tips of her breasts. "I don't want to fight either," she manages. "I want to..."

She doesn't finish so I do it for her. "Yeah. Me, too."

Another wave of heat rolls over her body, spurring a growl foreign to anything that resembles rage. "When this is over, let's pick up from here, and see where it takes us."

At her nod, I bend to kiss her.

My lips never make it to hers.

A powerful entity emerges from the shadows

And it attacks with the vengeance of a thousand fires.

CHAPTER TEN

"Get the hell off my sister!"

I don't get to see who the husky voice belongs to. Everything happens too fast.

The entire yard electrifies, standing my hair on its end. This is volatile magic, raw and unrepenting. My only thought is to haul Celia to safety, but there's no time. There's only pain and destruction.

Jolts of power strike down my nerve pathways and detonate at my core. I'm thrown across the property and slam-dunked into an old wood pile.

I fall into a seizure, all my cells convulsing with fire and pain. The severity of my jerks and twitches break apart the rotted wood I landed in and roll me to the ground.

More by instinct than any movement I purposely control, I shove away the magical charge. It's enough to allow me to crawl forward, even as I continue to jolt.

As the charge decreases to painful spurts of static shock, it occurs to me that I was struck by lightning.

Struck by lightning?

I push up on my arms, looking for Celia.

A young woman with dark hair and dressed in a tight black

T-shirt and leopard pajama pants hovers over a large, singed hole, the shape and outline of Celia.

Oh, *shit*.

Beside the brunette, another girl in gray sweatpants and a blue hoodie bounces in place, a baseball bat gripped tightly in her hand. Her slick black ponytail swings in all directions, given her frenzied state. It's then I'm sure Celia is buried in that damn hole.

I push up on my legs, only to crash land on my knees again. I don't even know what I'm doing here. I only know that Celia brought me and that I need to get to her.

"Dude," ponytail girl says. "You have to work on your aim. You zapped Celia. As in, fried her like chicken on the Fourth of July."

"Back off, Shayna," Leopard Pants says. "It was a total accident. Besides, I only zapped her a little bit. Look, she's already coming around, aren't you, Ceel?"

Celia makes this odd groaning noise.

"See?" Leopard Pants says. "She's fine."

What are they doing to her? I shake my head, trying to clear the fog clouding my reasoning. We weren't supposed to meet them here, were we?

I force myself to concentrate, trying to get a grasp on what's happening.

Another girl, this one really young with blond hair, steps onto the back porch. The light from the interior casts a halo around her, bleaching the strands of her wavy hair and her pastel blue nightgown.

"What happened?" she asks. She covers her mouth to stifle a scream. "Goodness, is that Celia?"

Leopard Pants rolls her eyes. "Who else would it be, Emme?" she asks her.

"A fricasseed piece of leftover streaker?" Shayna offers. She holds up her hands when Leopard Pants glares at her. "No, offense Taran, but what's left of her clothes are smoking and her hair is a little too high, even for Jersey."

Taran, the one in the leopard pants rams her hands on her hips. "Instead of knocking me down, you should be thanking me."

Emme drops her hand away. "For electrocuting Celia?" she asks.

"No. For electrocuting the perv who straddled her like a pony," Taran replies. She bats her hand away when Emme gasps. "It's okay, Emme. I fried his ass. He won't be back."

Little blond Emme inches forward. "Who was he?" she asks Taran.

Taran tosses back her hair. "I told you, some creepy bastard."

Nice. I push up on my legs, they're wobbly, but I manage not to fall again.

Emme ties the robe she's wearing. She appears exhausted, and was likely awoken by the commotion. Her hair is long like Celia's, but unlike Celia she's extremely timid and uncoordinated. She takes each step carefully, worried she'll fall despite the snow boots covering her feet.

"Celia? Are you alright?" She yelps when she gets a good look at her. "Is she having a seizure?" She leans in. "Oh, my, her sneakers are on fire."

Shayna spins her bat at her side. "Nah, Em. They're just smoking now. I kicked some dirt on her and put those flames right out."

"She looks awful." Emme grips the front of her robe. "Taran, what did you do to poor Celia?"

Celia groans, this time squeakier. I can't tell if she's better or worse. I manage to step forward despite the leftover jolts threatening to knock me back on my ass.

"Why is everything always my fault?" Taran demands. "I— *shit.* She *is* still on fire. Shayna, throw some more dirt on her." Celia starts coughing. "Not on her face, damn it. Her shoes— *her shoes.*"

"Taran," little Emme reprimands. "Celia just finished the last of those horrible shifts. You really need to be more careful with her."

"I told T the same thing, Em," Shayna agrees. She motions to Taran, who is so livid small lightning bolts crackle over her head. "But you know how T gets when she tries to"—she adds finger quotes—"help."

I slap my palm against the tree to keep my balance. *How is Celia still alive with these three around?*

"Damn it, Shayna, you make it sound like I did it on purpose," Taran quips. "Please, don't thank me for saving her life or anything."

Celia groans again, her hand lifting. She's not one to curse, but it's like she's trying to raise that one special finger to express her gratitude to Taran.

"Maybe I should try to heal her?" Emme asks. She bends at Celia's side, a soft yellow light sputters to life, enveloping Emme and adding to her ethereal appearance. "Don't worry, Celia. This shouldn't hurt, um, much."

Celia holds up her shaking hands, attempting to stop her. "No-no-no," she stammers.

These may be her sisters, but they've helped enough. "Get away from her," I roar.

I stomp forward.

Emme screams.

Shayna jumps up and down, pointing. "It's the perv! The one who humped Celia!"

"Attack!" Taran orders.

"No!" Celia leaps to her feet...and right into the path of Taran's lightning.

Taran curses as Celia is thrown into the neighboring yard. I tear after Celia, but only make it a few feet. I dive into the snow when a funnel of blue and white shoots toward me. Heat blisters my skin as the funnel expands and spreads over top of me.

I roll away and kick up to my feet. The two trees behind me are now on fire and Celia is nowhere to be found. "Are you crazy?" I demand.

Taran regards me like I'm the lunatic. "I told you to get away from her," she snaps.

Shayna skips forward. I don't mean she sprints. I'm saying she actually skips, her ponytail bouncing with each hop. If it's a distraction tactic, it doesn't quite work. She swings her bat with her wrist, each rotation elongating the wood and transforming it into a large metal sword that gleams silver in the moonlight.

Using the momentum of her motions, she flings the sword at me. I leap out of the way, roaring with pain as it goes through my leg and stakes me to the ground.

Shayna cheers. "I got him. I got the creepy guy." She stops celebrating when I wrench myself up and pull the sword free from my leg. It falls in the form of a warped piece of wood when I toss it on the ground. "Uh, oh," she says, backing away.

A clay pot smacks me in the shoulder. I slap away the broken pieces. "What the hell?" I snarl.

I dodge out of the way of the next load of garden supplies Emme flings at me, leaping behind a tree when a wheelbarrow jets at me and almost takes off my head. I edge out enough to see every remaining clay pot floating around Emme.

All right, little one, I see you. You're not so timid after all.

The pots jerk when I step away from the tree, her surprise to find me still alive affecting her confidence.

"Wh-why isn't he running away?" Emme stammers. "Shouldn't he be running away?"

"Because asshole here is too stupid to run," Taran tells her.

"*What?*" I growl.

Taran points at me. "Get him!" she shouts. "Show the little bitch what you're made of, Emme."

My presence and pissed-off demeanor further rattles Emme. She launches her pots. Her nervousness, though, makes her clumsy. I dodge every strike with ease, catching a few and stacking them beside me like a pyramid.

Shayna's jaw drops open. "Is he, like, mocking us?" She looks at Taran. "I think creepy dude is totally mocking us."

Taran scowls, annoyed. "Son of bitch," she mutters. "Do I have to do everything myself?"

She breathes in deep. As she breathes out, strobes of blue and white fire build in her hands.

I catch a bag of potting soil Emme throws and spin, launching the bag into Taran's chest when she fires. It's not a hard throw. It's just enough to knock the wind out of her and send the flaming strobes rolling into the neighboring yard.

I step over the singed lines of soil. So much for a neat yard. These three made a hot mess out of it, and, for the record, they still have not brought me down.

The scent of burning pine cuts through the aroma of fresh fallen snow. The trees Taran struck splinter and drop over, disintegrating as the flames continue to eat through the trunks.

Taran isn't all talk. She has the goods to cause some serious damage. But like the others, her power is sporadic and undeveloped.

Emme races to Taran's side, jumping when the bag of soil catches fire. "Son a bitch," Taran moans.

"Get up, Taran. Hurry," Emme urges, her eyes wide. "The perverted gentleman is still coming."

Shayna presses her foot into the aluminum door leading to the front porch and yanks on the knob. "I got this," she says. She elongates the knob, transforming into a dagger. She hurls it and...stabs Celia in the thigh with it.

Celia falls to ground, her clothes are in tatters, she's covered in dirt, and her hair is as big as a bush in spring. I pull her to a sitting position. "Are you all right, sweetness?"

Celia yanks the dagger from her leg and tosses it aside. Unlike the bat, it maintains its form. Her gaze is murderous as she takes in her sisters. *"Stop trying to kill my boyfriend,"* she growls.

Emme hooks her arms around Taran to try to lift her. She drops her, gaping at Celia. "B- boyfriend? Did you say he's your boyfriend?"

Shayna eyes the broom she picked and tries to hide it behind her. "Is that why you were having sex with him in the snow?"

I don't know whose face reddens faster, mine, Celia's, or Emme's. I take a good look at Emme who appears ready to bury herself in the snow. Definitely Emme.

"Watch what you say in front of the little girl," I warn. Emme may have come at me, but she's still just a kid.

"I'm sixteen," Emme insists.

"You are?" I ask, shocked.

"And we weren't having sex," Celia insists.

No. Not yet.

The memory of our contact sends ripples of lust to consume me, an easy task with Celia's body pressed tightly against mine. She shudders again and attempts to clear her throat. "This is Aric. He's a werewolf."

Taran sits up, her annoyance as obvious as the mini-bolts of lightning that crackle above her head. "Damn it, Celia, you're supposed to marry a doctor."

"*What*?" I ask.

Taran scoffs. "You heard me, *Blues Clues*." She motions around us. "You think we're killing ourselves in nursing school to run around naked every full moon? You think we want to give birth to puppies? Go back to your cave and bury a bone or something. We don't do animal sex around here."

Shayna holds up a finger. "That's actually an offensive stereotype, T."

"I don't give a shit," Taran says. She pushes herself up into a standing position. "Celia, a werewolf, really? We have enough against us. Do you really want to deal with crazies showing up on our doorstep trying to stake us?"

"Those are vampires," Shayna replies. She's trying to whisper and doing a terrible job. "And in all fairness, Celia never said she wanted to marry a doctor. Schuck's, given her dating history, we'll be lucky if she doesn't die a decrepit old virgin, with her barren uterus dangling to her toes."

Celia covers her face. "He can hear you," she hisses.

I laugh, kissing her along her neck and speaking low. "You're a virgin?"

"Um." It's all Celia says, but it's enough.

My humor fades. "I haven't taken a lover either," I admit. "I'd be honored to take you."

"Ah," Celia squeaks.

Taran rolls her eyes, oblivious to our conversation but mindful of the connection between us. "Fine. Your choice," Taran says. She dusts herself off. "*I'm* still marrying a doctor."

Shayna tilts her head. "You cold, Ceel?" she asks. "Your nipples are like, really pointy." She looks at Taran. "Do you ever remember Celia's nipples pointing north and northwest like that? I don't. You think you zapped her a little too hard?"

Taran does a double-take as the temperature between me and Celia shoots sky high. She flashes an evil smile. "Shayna, that's not my lightening. That's *Teen Wolf* over there and his titillating man parts."

Emme eases forward as I look for another bag of soil to fling at Taran. It's not that Taran isn't right about what she says about me and Celia, it's how hard Celia is searching for the nearest escape that bothers me.

"I-I'm Emme, Mr. Werewolf, sir," she says. She blushes again even though there's nothing to blush about. "I'm Celia's sister."

"It's just Aric," I say. I smile. She's already my favorite. "And I know who you are, Emme."

I adjust my hold on Celia. She's hurt and bleeding. I need to get her help, fast. "You need a doctor."

"No," Celia says. "Doctors are obliged to report evidence of assault. It doesn't look good that I'm stabbed and electrocuted." She gives Taran and Shayna the side eye. "Jersey isn't like your hometown, where *weres* and their mates coexist and magic is accepted. The police will be called, and I'll be questioned."

"I-I can heal you," Emme offers.

Celia's eyes round, but it's not from surprise. "Please don't."

"You're a healing witch?" I ask.

Taran slumps to her knees beside us. "She's not a witch, Hooch. None of us are." She waves off my concern when my attention returns to Emme. "Emme can heal herself just fine. She's just not good at healing others, you feel me?"

"I'm not *that* bad," Emme insists. "I'm learning."

"Not fast enough," Taran mutters. She tries to bat down Celia's giant poufy hair. I think she makes it worse.

Celia smacks her hands away. "Quit trying to help," she tells Taran. "You've done enough."

Taran falls back on her heels and surrounds herself in blue and white flame to keep warm. "Ceel, come on. When I saw you getting it on, I didn't realize it was consensual. You haven't had a date since…" She snaps her fingers to get Shayna's attention.

"Oh, it's been like *years*, dude," Shayna answers.

"Oh, *God*," Celia mumbles.

"Remember?" Shayna asks. "That guy with the unibrow she went out with?" Emme and Taran shake their heads. "You know, the Lord of the Rings fan who showed up in that Hobbit costume?"

Taran gives it some thought. "Are you talking about that freak from the grocery store?"

"No," Shayna says. "I'm talking about the one with the disgusting hairy feet."

"Those were real?" Emme asks. "I thought it was part of his elfwear."

"*Hobbit*," Shayna clarifies.

"Oh, yeah, him," Taran says, ignoring Celia's death glare. "He looked nasty. He smelled nasty. He *was* nasty. You could have braided all that shit covering his feet. And why the fuck was he barefoot?"

"No clue," Shayna tells her. She stands and pats my back. "Anyway, don't worry about it, Wolfman. Hobbit guy dumped Celia halfway through dinner when he realized she didn't speak Elvish." She tosses a broken pot into the wheelbarrow. "It was totally humiliating. But we've moved past it, haven't we, Ceel?"

Celia doesn't reply, unless you count her burying her flaming face deeper in her hands.

Taran leans in. I don't stop her because her fire is keeping Celia warm. "Did you at least use protection?" she asks, like I'm not right here. "Not with that Frodo loser, but with Howl-at-the-Moon, here?" She blinks back at Celia when Celia's jaw pops open. "Don't look at me like that. I don't know much about werewolves. All I know is they like to get naked and knock up women with their giant c—"

"*Taran, zip it*," Celia warns.

Shayna stops trying to straighten the yard and skips over to us, tilting her chin when she takes another look at Celia. "Did you get hit in the neck? You have like, all these bruises on your neck—Oh. Never mind, they're hickies." She turns to Emme. "I think you should try to heal her. Celia may have thicker skin than we do but the stab wound is pretty deep. If it gets infected, she'll have to go to the hospital for sutures."

Celia looks up at me. "I'll be okay. I just need a moment."

"I think you need more than that," I rumble. I'm not thrilled with the idea of Emme trying to heal her. I've seen her fight and her abilities are clumsy at best. "What are the chances of you losing your limbs if Emme tries to heal you?"

Shayna laughs. "C'mon, Derrick, Emme's not *that* bad."

"It's Aric," I remind her.

"Whatever." Taran rolls her eyes. "Like this shit's gonna last."

"Knock it off," Celia growls at her. She frowns. "Why are you smiling?" she asks me.

I adjust my hold to better see her face. "They don't think we'll make it. I'm willing to prove them wrong." My smirk dissolves. "No matter how much time we have."

Celia quiets.

"What's that supposed to mean?" Taran asks.

Celia glances down, attempting to hide her feelings. "Aric is only here for a little while," she explains. "But I don't want to talk about it."

I don't want to think about our limited time together, either. Celia is the only thing I'm worried about now. She winces when I stroke the slope of her side.

"What's wrong?" I ask her.

My fingers press along her ribs when she doesn't answer, examining each bone. "Celia, at least two of your ribs are broken."

She crinkles her nose. "I figured," she says.

The curses that fly out of my mouth aren't anything she's used to. I don't mean to upset her. I just had no idea how bad she was hurt. "Why didn't you tell me? You've been running with the injuries and jumping all over hell." I glance back to the neighboring property. "You *flipped* over those cinderblocks."

"Aric, I'm used to pain." She smiles a little. "And regardless of what you think, I'm a lot tougher than I look."

"I tackled you," I remind her.

"You did?" Emme asks.

"Oh, totally," Shayna says. "It was like a lion in the Serengeti and Ceel was the zebra."

"Are you serious?" Emme asks.

We're blushing like teens caught by their parents, though no one seems to care.

Taran rolls her eyes, again. "What part of they-were-doing-it-like-wildebeests didn't you understand?"

"He was really gentle about it," Celia stammers.

"I still could have hurt you," I remind her.

She looks at me, red-faced. "No. You'd never hurt me."

No, I wouldn't. I kiss her temple; happy she knows it, but worried all the same. Celia can't keep going like this. "You need help healing, sweetness. Will you let Emme help you?"

"Aric, I know this sounds good in theory, but Emme is able to feel what she's healing. She starts off well but the more she feels, the more nervous she gets. It slows the process and makes it more um, uncomfortable."

She offers Emme an apologetic glance. Emme is looking too hard at the ground to notice.

As much as Celia was trying to spare her feelings, it only heightened my concern.

I rub my jaw, trying to suppress the emotions I'm experiencing. Celia is used to pain no one has any right to endure. Between the throwdown with the pack and her sisters' collective efforts to save her, Celia is worse off, hurting more than she's letting on.

Now that I'm aware, my wolf and I can sense her pain. Man, she's strong. It will take a lot to bring her down. That doesn't mean I want her to suffer.

"Sweetness, I know this isn't our best option. But if it's ultimately to your benefit, I think you should do it."

"Please, baby," I add when she hesitates. "Do it for me."

Celia glances down. "All right," she agrees. She lifts her gaze to take me in. "It's going to hurt. Emme isn't very fast. Just don't freak out, okay? I'll muscle through it."

I start having second thoughts when I realize how scared she seems. Damn. She wasn't this scared of Odin. "How much pain are we talking here?" I ask.

"Oh, depending how deep Emme has to go to put Ceel back in fighting shape, a lot," Shayna explains.

"A good healing witch wouldn't cause you much pain," I say aloud.

Taran looks at Celia. This time there's no attitude, just enough sadness to demonstrate she is human after all. "Like I said, we're not witches. We're just us."

Emme regards Celia as if already apologizing ahead of time. "Are you ready, Celia?

"Yes," Celia agrees.

"You want her to heal those hickies, too?" Shayna asks.

"*Yes, Shayna,*" Celia grinds out.

I nod at Emme. "Just be careful with her, all right?"

Emme's voice is as soft as the snowflakes that start to form. "I'll do my best, Aric," she promises.

I keep my arms wrapped around Celia. I'm unsure if I'm supposed to, except I'm not willing to let her go.

Emme's pale yellow light sputters to life and surrounds her. Using care, she places her hands over Celia's head.

It's then that evil awakens, and all hell breaks loose.

Chapter Eleven

Thunder cracks and wind gusts arrive full force, sweeping the dense layers of snow and debris all over the yard.

Emme's light cocoons me as I clutch Celia tighter. I try to shield her from the flying fragments, but we're being pegged from all directions.

Celia arches her back, her nails protruding to rake along the snow as agony consumes her. With a jolt, I realize her response isn't only from Emme healing her. Nor is this magical assault a result of Emme's power.

My purpose for being here cracks me hard across the head. The evil, the one we seek, has arrived. Between the gusts, its sinister whisper warns me to run or die.

I'm not going anywhere.

And this thing is what's going to die

Emme screams, jerking away from Celia. "Something bad is here," she stammers. Slowly, she turns in the direction of the house. "I think it's coming for us."

Her pale-yellow light flickers in and out. She curls inward, shaking. I snag her arm and pull her back to Celia.

"Emme, you have to finish healing, Celia," I yell over the howling wind. "Do you hear me? Whatever you do, don't stop. This thing will come after her while she's vulnerable."

Emme nods, her understanding fueling her magic.

Shayna shields her eyes; the increasing wind is kicking up rubble and making it hard to see. "I feel something, too. I'm just not sure what it is," she says. She lifts the broom from the ground. "There's bad juju like, everywhere. We need to get Celia inside where it's safe."

"No," I insist. "That's what it wants you to think. Whatever this thing is hatched inside and is extending its magic outward."

"Hatching" doesn't paint a pretty picture and it reflects across Shayna's pixie features. "Dude. Are you serious?" she asks.

"Of course, I am," I yell over the bedlam. "And whatever it is, it's trying to finish what it started."

Shayna clutches the broom tighter to her body. She may not fully understand, but she's readying for a fight.

Thunder erupts, shaking the ground and rattling the windows across several homes.

"What the hell is happening?" Taran snaps. "You don't get to just show up and tell us shit like this."

Sweat pours down Celia's scrunching face. She may be in pain, but she also remembers. Emme's ability to heal must have destroyed the veil blinding us to the truth. Everything that's happened to her and her family hits Celia at once.

"Taran, Aric's right," Celia manages through clenched teeth. "We have to stop it."

She tries to rise, but I ease her back down. "No," I tell her. "You're too weak. Let Emme finish mending you."

Taran drops to her knees beside her. "Celia, tell me what's going on."

"Something evil has taken over our home," Celia tells her. Her body jerks and she kicks out her feet in her pain. "It's been leeching our souls for months. It's why Aric is here. He's trying to help us."

Taran's hair whips in all directions. She turns toward the house. "We have to get Ana Lisa out of there!"

"No!" I snatch Taran's wrist before she can bolt. "I need you to stay here until Celia's healed, you hear me?"

She yells over the sweeping wind, her eyes wild. "No! You don't get to call the shots."

"Yes, I do." My snarl shuts her up. "Celia's down. Your sisters need you. *I* need to get in there and destroy whatever caused all this."

Taran turns back toward the house, igniting a piece of fencing that soars toward us with fire. It explodes and so does Taran. "You're nothing to us, werewolf," she accuses. "Why should we listen to you?"

I'm ready to answer her rage with mine. Instead, I squeeze Celia's hand.

In her warmth and spirit, I am the male I wish to become. I press a kiss along her knuckles, permitting our connection to steady me and comfort her through her torment.

"I may be nothing to you," I tell Taran. "But Celia is *everything* to me."

Shayna gasps and cuts her gaze toward Taran. "I think he means it, T."

Taran, despite her resentment of me, falls perfectly still.

"She's hurt, Taran," I tell her. "Celia can't fight. You can. I need you to take out anything that comes at you."

"Okay. *Fine*," Taran grinds out. She's not crazy about me ordering her around.

Fair enough. I've seen them fight. I'm not exactly nuts about leaving them in charge.

The sky erupts in a wash of red. We're out of time. My wolf ravages to the surface. He's ready to fight and do what must be done. Except it's not quite time for him to appear.

Sometimes a wolf needs the man more.

The magic doubles and that sense of wrongness thickens the current, making it hard to breathe. "Where are you?" I growl.

Evil responds, and it doesn't like me calling it out.

A beam of bright red punches through the sky and splits the tree in half. I lift Celia, rushing her away from the falling branches.

I don't get far when the ground rumbles beneath us. I keep my feet. So does Emme, but Taran and Shayna are knocked to the ground. I start toward them, only managing a few steps.

Red lines puncture from the roots of the demolished tree and ripple across the earth, breaking up the soil and encircling the property. Another jolt, another hard shake. Emme hangs tight to Celia's arm, her pale-yellow light faltering as she fights to keep her magic and her balance. The others aren't so fortunate.

"Get out of here, now!" I yell.

Taran topples over Shayna. "Son of a bitch, we're trying!' Taran fires back.

She and Shayna don't quite make it to their feet when heavy chains ribboned with fire bust through the mangled yard and up. They crisscross in the sky, forming a star.

"Oh, fuck," Taran mumbles. "This can't be good."

It's not.

Clouds as red as blood swirl together, latching onto each point and creating a pentagram coloring everything beneath it an unsettling shade of red.

As the disturbing red light washes over us, strange symbols appear against our skin. The pentagram spins, strengthening the force of the wind and turning it deadlier.

Rocks, dirt, *anything* littering the ground pelts us from all directions. I haul Emme on top of Celia, followed by Shayna and Taran. I'm last, protecting them with my body.

Emme's light pokes through, challenging the sick red glow as she adds more power.

She knows her light can lift the veil and make her sisters see.

I lift up from them, punching the cinderblock flying toward us into rubble.

"Taran, can you surround your sisters with fire without burning them?" I shake her when she doesn't answer me. "*Taran*."

"I feel it," she says. "That thing that's in there."

She's crying. I hear it in her voice and sense it in her demeanor.

"I can too, T," Shayna says. She's about as composed as Taran. They're all losing it based on the months this thing has leeched from them.

"It's okay," I tell them. "I'm going inside to kill it."

"Kill what, exactly, dude?" Shayna asks. "You said it's magic. How do you kill magic?"

If my hearing wasn't as keen as it is, I wouldn't be able to hear them over the churning wind and all the flying debris. I speak loudly, over the wind and sounds of destruction. "If I can destroy the spell, I'll eliminate the magic it created, and any creature born of it."

"You know how to destroy a spell, werewolf?" Taran asks.

Not all, but enough. "Yes. Just keep each other safe, all right?" I remember what Celia said to me. "Just like she's always done for you."

Taran nods. She gets it. "Okay, werewolf," she replies.

I edge away, hoping the aggression she meets me with will help her to combat this power. The cyclone within the perimeter picks up speed, the malevolent magic surging. It's trying to amp up whatever is in the house.

I'm amped up, too.

I punch through the broken shutters the wind rips from the house and fling away a heavy branch that flies at us. The branch collides against the wall of red light, splintering it like glass. It doesn't break through the shield, but it shows me it's not indestructible. The girls may be able to charge through it if they have to.

With a growl I push on, my lids lowered to protect my eyes from the dirt peppering the air. We're being bombarded from all directions, the noise alone enough to scramble my senses. I urge my wolf, bringing him as close to the surface as I can without *changing* to keep me oriented.

It takes me smashing through flying fencing and more branches before it's finally safe for Taran to stand. The wind is wicked, striking us so hard, she barely keeps her balance.

Taran screams. I think she's scared and won't make it. But then she curses, slams her fists into the ground and screams again.

Blue and white flames cut into the beat-up earth, encircling Taran and her sisters. The ribbon of flames spiral upward, forming a fiery tornado that shelters them in.

A lawn chair strikes the edge of the tornado. The dark magic challenging Taran's light. Taran raises her middle finger, watching the chair melt into a warped piece of garbage.

I don't know this young woman. They could be safe for a long while or they may only have moments. I plan to use every second they can spare. Except this thing is worse than I ever imagined. Inexperienced or not, Celia and her sisters have a catacomb of power that's nourished the evil within.

I cover my face with my arm, leaving just enough space to look at Celia as if it's our final goodbye. Emme's telekinesis works immediately, her healing ability though is arduously slow. Celia isn't making a sound. I recognize her pain in her crinkled brow and how she stiffens beneath Emme's touch.

"If I don't make it, run," I tell Taran. "Use your fire to break your way out."

Taran looks in the direction of the house and to a corner room. Their foster mother is there. I can tell by the way she appears torn. But then she turns in the direction of the cracked shield and nods.

Shayna, watching us, pushes to her feet. She extends the arm holding the broom upward. Using her ability, she transforms the broom it into a long and deadly sword. Its slick blade reflects Taran's fire. "You better make it, dude," she says. She motions to Celia, writhing in pain beneath Emme's touch. "I think my sister really likes you."

Over the roar of the cyclone, I speak my truth. "I really like her, too."

My forearm crunches when I smack the busted tree trunk that flies at me. I aim for the shield and nail it. The base splinters and branches up, creating enough of a split that the girls should be able to break through.

Taran and Shayna gasp when my arm falls limp to the side. It hurts. I'm not invincible. But like Taran continues to point out, I am a werewolf. In the few seconds I use to roll my arm and stretch it, is all it takes for my wolf to repair the bone and mend the tissue.

I start for the back steps only for my wolf to warn against it. He jerks our focus to the corner room where Ana Lisa, the woman who fostered and raised my Celia, waits. I take off in a sprint, crashing through the window and landing in a crouch.

Chapter Twelve

The house is spared from the discord outside. If the neighbors share the same fortune, it will keep them safely inside and away from the chaos.

Broken glass slides off my shoulders in large pieces as I rise. Aside from the crinkling sound it makes as it hits the floor, there's no sound save one.

Ana Lisa lies to my left. My arrival didn't stir her from sleep. But then it's hard to wake those so close to death.

Her pained breathing speaks in a way that words cannot. There's a lot behind each breath: hurt and regret, but also courage. Ana Lisa fights for her life, refusing to allow death to easily claim her.

In a picture beside her bed, a heavy-set black woman laughs as two little girls struggle to fit on her lap. The black ponytail and blond curls give away that it's Shayna and Emme despite that their profiles are barely visible.

Behind them, Taran rolls her eyes, her hand on Ana Lisa's shoulder. Her attitude remains firmly in place, but her touch gives away her devotion.

My Celia stands behind Ana Lisa, watching over her family as she's done all her life. Emme and Shayna have changed so much. Taran has, too. Celia, despite appearing younger, hasn't changed as much. The stealthy determination she carries is evident, as is her sadness.

The one most changed lies in bed, suffering with each breath she takes.

Gray, loose skin covers what remains of Ana Lisa's cancer-ridden body. She isn't moving, and her struggle to keep breathing is as blatant as her illness. Her gaunt and strained features remind me of my mother. But Mom's wolf has kept her in far better health than Ana Lisa's spirit.

Mom wants to join my father in death. Her heart is broken as well as her soul.

Ana Lisa, so sick and weak, fights this evil with her soul and heart. It doesn't matter that she doesn't have an inner beast to help her. Here she lies, battling it out for her babies.

This human woman's grit inspires my resolve. Whatever it takes, I'm determined to enliven my mother's spirit so her wolf can heal them. All Mom needs is something to motivate her. Ana Lisa needs so much more. Regardless, these women deserve to live. Nothing will stop me from saving them.

The last few shards of glass fall away as I carefully take in the room. My break-in was savage but the cuts to my skin are only minor. My wolf heals me with little effort despite my overwhelming need for food.

From my periphery, a shadowy figure with long, spindly fingers slips behind an old wooden desk. Another scurries behind a tall dresser where a television broadcasts a political debate. They're fast. I'm unsure a human would have spotted them even now.

I sniff the air to be certain what they are. The aroma of dark licorice dipped in tar has me scrunching my nose.

Nullits. I sniff again. Yeah. That's what they are. Their unique ability to null their victims' senses permits them to go unnoticed until it's too late, hence the name. They can hide in the open if they maintain their flat forms and keep to the shadows. It makes it easy for them to feed on their victims' souls and multiply quickly.

I'm surprised to find them here. The spell that raises them is complex. Only a powerful witch can cast it. If done incorrectly, it can turn on its wielder. When done right, it's an effective and tortuous way to take down the enemy.

"Enemy." I mull over the word, beating back a growl. This isn't merely a curse to avenge an insult. Whoever targeted this family *hates* them. Cruel and meant to kill slowly, the spell is outlawed in all corners of the earth. To cast it equates to an automatic death sentence. Yet here it is, slowly killing my love and her family.

I mutter a curse when I catch sight of a youngling scamper beneath the ceiling fan. My stomach sours. These things are actively breeding. It will make taking them out harder. Like roaches, it just takes one to live for a new batch to hatch. With Celia and her sisters as powerful as they are, the nullits have reproduced in great numbers. My wolf picks up on several just inside the room. He snaps his jaws, eager to stalk and have us destroy them.

I ease to a crouch, scanning the area for the best line of attack and alert to any hint of movement.

Nullits start out small, about the size of my calf. Like newborns, they're voracious eaters, growing from tormenting their prey and feasting on their wounded souls. Depending on the circumstances and the number of victims, it may only take weeks for them to reach adulthood. That's when they're most lethal and cause the greatest anguish.

I step toward the bed, breathing in the medicine coated room. Several nullits wait on the other side. But something bigger is hiding in the closet. It's hungry, and well into adulthood. It could be the first born from the spell, or it could have leeched from the strongest family member of all.

Celia.

My Celia.

There's no suppressing my growls now.

These creatures, all of them, have been robbing this family of their lives and relishing in their pain. I want to tear them to pieces. If I get them, all of them, the girls will recover with time. Ana Lisa won't. For her, this wonderful woman who took in these girls no one else wanted, it's too late.

The cancer, and the chemo permeating through her graying skin, have incapacitated her. With the nullits gone, her health will slightly improve. She'll have more time, maybe another few months, but not more than that.

The click-clack sounds beneath the bed draw my attention. The nullits are taunting my beast, daring us to investigate.

No worries. We will, in time.

Closet first.

I move slowly, catching sight of a shadowy hand that disappears beneath the bed, the long thin fingers more like claws than digits. The hasty motion and its desire to draw my attention leave marks along the wood.

Hmph. This thing really wants me under the bed. Fine. We'll play its game when I'm ready. Right now, I make the rules.

The room isn't big, just large enough for an antique bed, a nightstand, the dresser, and desk. It's not an ideal place to fight. The advantage is there are few places for these things to hide. I round the bed as if I'm headed to the other side. I change direction quickly, throwing open the closet door and reaching in.

My hand snags what feels like hard stretched rubber. I yank a nullit as tall as me by the arm and twist, securing it and the opposite wrist.

We're taught to fight many types of supernatural creatures. We've also studied weaknesses and strengths from those born of spells. Nullits suck on souls and magic through multiple mouths.

Yes, *multiple* mouths. On faces, hands, and feet.

The red, sticky lips on the nullit's palm drool and eagerly slurp, desperate to lick and taste my magic. I do as I told Celia. I shove the malevolent energy away, effectively blocking it from feeding on me.

Nullits, while able to flatten into shadows, are pliable and slick in their solid form. They don't possess bones or joints, permitting them to adjust into any position for an optimal feed.

I twist the nullit around, locking its limbs around its own chest. Decapitation works on many supernaturals. It would work on this creature if its form wasn't so malleable. I search for a weapon, spotting a standing lamp near the corner.

It's exactly what I need. I release the nullit long enough to grab the lamp.

The nullit is damn fast. I'm faster. I secure the metal rod of the lamp against its throat and pull.

Most supernatural creatures tend to abhor metals.

Weres and vamps, gold.

Demons and spirits, silver.

Nullits are no exception. The metallic rod burns through its throat. It should be a quick kill. It's not. This one is strong and wants to drain me dead.

It slams me against the wall. I hang tight, grunting with the effort. Like burning through a truck tire with a lighter, it takes time to cut my way through.

The nullit flails as I drive the rod deeper. It thrusts me into the dresser, sending the television crashing to the floor. I kick away from the wall when it tries to mash me through it, my frustration helping me pull tighter.

Its fear makes it angry and more vicious. It swats at me, trying to reach me without touching the rod. The fingers slash my skin, leaving lesions that sizzle like acid. I push aside the sting and focus, allowing the nullit to swing me around and spare my energy. This is the first and many more await.

I concentrated my strength into my arms and use my weight to drag the rod closer to my body. I'm almost through when the Nullit under the desk snags my ankle.

I fall purposely backward, bending the Nullit's spine and snapping the rod against its throat. I stomp the other Nullit as I land, but not before its claws rake across my calf and sever my Achilles tendon.

The first nullit's head breaks away, exploding into a puff a smoke. The rest of its body follows, meeting the same fate.

The nullit who sliced my tendon circles me, the mouths on its face and hands smacking in anticipation of a feed. I kick it away when it pounces. It strikes the wall and shrieks. With lethal speed, it rebounds and leaps into the air.

Its lack of strategy and greed work against it. I snatch the rod from the floor and push it up as the nullit lands. Its weight and speed make it easy for the rod to pierce the nullit's torso.

Its high-pitched screams rattle the window. I think I hear Celia's voice in the distance, speaking fast. I push the thought aside, hoping she's well enough to take her family to safety.

The metal splits the nullit in half, the two sections that break away vanishing before they hit the floor.

I'm not yet to my feet when several hands reach from beneath the bed and try to pull me under. I snag both pieces of rod and stab the creatures under the bed with the sharp ends.

One stab. Two stabs. Three stabs. *Die.*

They screech, their shadowy forms dissolving into the air. Ana Lisa jerks up, moaning with pain and fear. They were the ones feeding from her. I'm glad to interrupt.

Another nullit dives from the ceiling. I clutch it by the throat but fail to control it. It's large and heavy and knocks me to the floor. I get my feet under it and lock them around its waist. With a turn of my hips, I roll it onto its back and stab it with my weapon.

As it fades, I rush to my feet to check on Ana Lisa. She's sitting up, clutching her throat.

"It's okay," I tell her. "I'm here to help."

She points, her eyes wild. My fist connects with a nullit who leaps from its spot on the wall. I nail it in the side of the head and send it scampering under the bed.

I barely make it to Ana Lisa when a Nullit springs from the shadows in the corner and forces me through the bedroom door. We land in the hallway, both of us gunning to kill.

The nullits I fought left deep scratches along my chest. My wolf rushed to heal them ahead of my tendon to protect my heart. I kick at the floor, my one foot useless as I drive the nullit away from the bedroom.

The injured nullits will pounce on Ana Lisa to nourish their bodies. I need to kill this one fast and get back to the others if she's to survive.

A few feet away, a small light in the bathroom illuminates the hall. Nullits don't like metal. They also don't like anything pure like water. Sounds like the place to go.

I kick my heels into the floor, charging my wolf with mending my tendon. My hands whip around the nullit, struggling to control its swinging limbs. This thing is smarter than the others. It's also stronger. Its famished mouths pucker frantically, hell-bent on draining me of my soul.

My foot snaps into place in one harsh move. I ignore the sharp pain and slam the nullit's limbs into its face. It stuns it long enough for me to get to my feet and drag it down the hall.

It screeches when it sees where we're headed and tries to pull away from me. I head butt it twice, stunning it again and wrenching it forward. An old cast iron tub runs along the checkerboard black and white tiled wall. I kick at the faucet, springing the overhead shower head to life.

The Nullit's shriek cracks the frosted glass window above the tub. It's scared and begging for mercy. After what it's done to Celia and her family, wrath is the only grace I have.

I thrust its body against the wall, indenting the tile and keeping it in place as I reach for the detachable shower head. I wrap the hose around its neck and kick the lever that starts the flow. The nullit shakes, falling into a seizure.

I leap out of the shower, breathing hard. I turn the water on faster when Celia appears.

"*Aric*!"

I catch her in my arms as she races forward. "What are you doing here?" I demand. "You should have run."

"I couldn't abandon you or Ana Lisa." She should be angry. Except all she does is take a moment to hold me as if I might slip away. "You're mine to protect."

My hand slides down her back as her words pull at my heart. *How will I live without you?*

She jerks away from the tub when the nullit releases another mind jolting shriek. I try to shield her from the sight. She sees it anyway.

"They're all over the house," I explain. "Some big, others small."

She watches in horror as an arm falls away. The mouth on the palm shrieks one last time before its abruptly silenced.

"*That's* what's been leeching our souls?" she asks.

I nod. "They don't like water or metal. Decapitation also works."

"Good to know," Celia says, her husky voice firm. Her tigress eyes flash. She understands what must be done and her beast is looking forward to it.

"Dude!" Shayna yells. She stumbles into the bathroom and almost drops her sword when she sees the last few pieces of the Nullit break away and fade. "Ceel, what is that?"

"A nullit," I say. "They're the creatures who've been feasting on you."

"They can be killed with metal or water," Celia adds. She gives Shayna a look. "You can also cut their heads off."

"On it," Shayna says and...skips away. "T, Em'," she hollers from the hall. "Things with bad haircuts have invaded the house."

"*What*?" Taran yells.

I pinch the bridge of my nose. *How are these girls still alive?*

"Nullits, Shayna," Celia calls out, her expression apologetic. "Not mullets."

We charge out of the bathroom when Emme and Taran scream. I get slightly ahead of Celia in time to watch Shayna lift her sword and spin across the kitchen like figure skater. As smooth as silk waving in the breeze, she decapitates three nullits cornering Taran and Emme.

I body slam the nullit that hurtles itself from the top of the refrigerator and crack it over the head with a pitcher of water. The water sizzles through its face and neck, killing it.

The nullit that springs from the floor encounters Celia's rage. Like a pendulum, Celia swipes her extended claws back and forth. The nullit doesn't have time to cry out. It collapses, convulsing and disappearing in an explosion of smoke. I snatch a charging nullit in a headlock and shove it beneath the kitchen sink, slapping the water on full blast.

At the same moment, Celia kicks the handle of a pot on the floor. She catches it as it spins upward and strikes it across a charging nullit's head, caving it inward. Her claws extend further, the muscles along her arms tensing as she slashes the nullit's throat, killing it.

Nullits don't like anything pure. I'm uncertain how Celia strikes it down with such ease. I won't worry about it now. I'm simply grateful she can protect herself.

Rat-like shrieking erupts from all directions. Nullits in all shapes and sizes materialize from the dark corners of the kitchen, beneath the kitchen table, and from behind furniture in the small family room. Celia races ahead, her sharp nails protruding as she flips over the couch and rams her nails into a nullit's chest.

"They don't like metal or water," Celia yells over her shoulder.

"How do they feel about fire?" Taran asks.

It's her dead tone voice that has me glancing back.

"Oh, *shit*."

I tackle Celia when Taran lets loose. Fire as bright as lava zooms over me and into a box-shaped nullit. The nullit crashes into the fireplace and detonates from the force of the blue and white flames.

The fire alarms blast in warning. I'm expecting the house to come down, but Taran controls the fire well enough, and the alarms quickly silence.

Celia and I scramble to our feet, her clawing at anything within her reach and me ramming a fire poker I seize through heads, chests, and stomachs.

Shayna scrambles on top of the island and, with the most pathetic warrior princess yell I've ever heard, lifts her sword and stabs the nullits scrambling across the ceiling.

I race toward Emme when a small group of nullits rush her. I barely acknowledge a rattling noise when multiple drawers fly open and every utensil in the kitchen jets out. Like a fountain of metal, Emme slices and dices every nullit stupid enough to mess with her.

Okay. Now, I see how they survived.

Taran walks forward, flames encircling the length of her arms. Her blue eyes blanche to white as she embraces the nullit like a lover. The nullit trembles, trying to break her hold.

Taran holds tight. "Die you son of bitch," she whispers.

The nullit explodes in a cloud, invading the small space. Taran doesn't move. She's angry and in her own head. Celia hurries to her. I'm worried Taran will burn her, but as she reaches for her sister's hand, the flames die out.

"Come on, Taran," she tells her. "Let's get Ana Lisa out of the house."

With one look, my love urges me to stay with her younger sisters. I do, believing most of the nullits have rushed to the immediate area.

I'm proven wrong when Taran releases a blood curling scream and the connection I feel to Celia abruptly vanishes.

Fear, unlike anything I've ever felt, rattles me down to my core. I take off down the hall, propelled by my wolf and the fear that Celia is gone.

Taran kneels on the bed, holding Ana Lisa's slumped form. A large burn mark stains the mirror and the opposite wall. Taran points to the foot of the bed, her olive skin ash. "They-they took Celia."

I shove the bed against the wall, using just enough care not to topple it over. An icy chill drags along my spine as I fix on the hell mouth before me.

A hole, as wide as the bed and as deep as a football field, sputters to life in that wicked red glow. At the base, a smaller pentagram glares obscene light, illuminating the hundreds of nullits crawling along the sides. They smack and scurry over each other, fighting to reach the unmoving form at the bottom.

"*Celia!*"

The pentagram casts enough light to shine across her terrified face. Nullits pile on top of her, brutalizing each other for a chance to feed from Celia's soul.

A naked man and a woman with no eyes and blood seeping from the large wounds on their chests crawl beside her, stroking her hair and whispering words I can't hear. Celia covers her face, sobbing, every emotion she feels engorging the nearby nullits.

There's no plan.

No hesitation.

No *fucking* way I'll let them take her from me.

I dive headfirst into that hell hole. I flip to soften the impact, except the hole is too deep and I break my leg as I land. The pain is nothing. I roll to Celia and gather her against me, kicking the nullits closest to her away with my broken leg.

They hiss at me with their mouths. I growl, warning them to keep away.

Celia cries into my chest, pointing at the people missing their eyes.

"It's an illusion, baby," I say. "Do you hear me, sweetness? They're not real."

"I see them," she stammers. "They're dead because of me."

"No," I answer, trying to keep the bite from my voice. "It's the spell. It uses your worst memories to break you so the nullits can attack and feed from you."

I glare at the versions of her mother and father. They smile at me. They think they have Celia where they want her.

They never counted on me.

From above me, the Wird girls scream.

The spell must be magnifying the illusion. It's the only way they can see it from here. "They're not real!" I yell, my voice thunderous. "They're trying to feed from your spirits and your magic. Don't let them. They can't hurt you if you don't let them."

My voice is softer when I address Celia. I stroke away her tears and kiss her face. "You hear me, sweetness? They're not real. I am. Stay with me, and I'll get you out.'"

Celia is shaking so violently I doubt she can hear me. Yet she nods, gripping my arm when I offer it to her. My knee and leg aren't finished realigning. I don't wait and start my ascent.

The nullits crawling along the walls become nothing more than rails on a ladder. I use them to climb. They're too stupid and so afraid of falling, they cling tight. I toss them over my shoulder when I'm done with them or kick their heads off when I push up.

These are young and too weak to leave their womb. They need nourishment before they can invade the home. They fed from Ana Lisa. All of them. It's a miracle she's still alive.

Their young ages make them easy to kill. It doesn't mean they're not dangerous and greedy. As small as they are, their combined efforts caused Celia's suffering and permitted them to eat.

I don't pity these parasites. I only want them gone.

"Push them away with your mind like I taught you," I say.

She clutches my arm tighter, saying nothing. I glance down to make sure she's all right. Her tigress eyes blink back at me. She's fighting. That's my girl. Except as long as she's here she's susceptible. I start to return my gaze upward when my wolf growls inside me.

Shayna and Emme wait only a few feet above me, their faces shiny with tears. They're speaking to us. Despite my keen senses, I can't hear over the bleating nullits.

Shayna extends her hand. My wolf growls again, but it's not directed at her.

Smaller nullits emerge from the center of the pentagram. They scurry away from the center like ants, revealing a piece of wood buried beneath. As I look closer, I realize the pentagram and the small symbols surrounding it are carved into the wood. *That's* the origin of the spell.

"Celia," I say. "Go to your sisters. I have something to do."

I lift her enough for Shayna to grab her hand and for Emme to use her telekinesis to pull her up. As soon as she's safe, I drop back down.

I land in a roll that spares my legs. I slap and kick away the nullits scrambling to shield the old piece of wood.

The wood burns and blisters my hands when I lift it, but I don't dare let go. I break it against my knee with one good strike, shattering the spell.

I expect a dramatic end. The explosion of sound and creatures dying or the pit caving in from all sides and trapping me.

There's only the sudden silence of a ruptured spell and the pure aroma of vanquished evil.

I stand in the center of the room, holding the smoldering pieces of broken wood and taking in the destruction the home miraculously withstood.

It's over. The spell is broken and the nullits are destroyed.

I only wish Celia and her family were as easily fixed.

Taran remains on the bed, holding Ana Lisa. I thought the nullits had finished off their foster mother. But she's still alive, her breathing steady and sleeping soundly.

Taran cries into her hands. Like the others, she saw more than enough.

Celia holds Emme and Shayna tucked under each arm. They sob, unable to control their grief. Tears streak Celia's bloody cheeks. She was hurt during the fight. Still, the scratches are nothing compared to her pain.

I take a knee in front of her, wishing I could hide her away from the creatures far worse than nullits, and all those bastards that will no doubt come for her.

But I can't.

Just as know I can't stay.

My head touches hers. "I love you," I say.

"I love you, too," she whispers. More tears flood her eyes. "Is it over?"

"Yes," I say.

She presses her lips to beat back her sorrow. It doesn't help. "Aric, those were our parents.

I know.

I stroke away a strand of blood-coated hair. "I'll be back. Don't worry. This won't take long."

She tries to rise. Her sisters tighten their hold, afraid to let her go.

They need her.

I need her to be safe.

"Where are you going?" she asks.

My voice is more beast than man. "You were cursed. I'm going find the witch responsible and make her pay with blood."

Chapter Thirteen

Odin's gray SUV careens down Route 22, slush kicking up at the window as he swerves left and right.

He almost lost control, again. I think this is the fifth, maybe the sixth time. I don't care. I only care that he gets me where I need to be.

A growl I've suppressed for too long vibrates along my throat when I see the sign: The Plainfields.

"How many cities carry this name?" I ask.

Odin glances my way, careful to avoid eye contact with me. "Three, Alpha. North Plainfield, Plainfield, and South Plainfield." He cuts right onto a small ramp. "This here right now is North Plainfield," he says. "Plainfield's where we're headed."

We slide down the small incline and through a red light. Brakes are a joke in this weather, not that it matters. There are no cars in sight. Only the desperate and those out for revenge dare to drive in this weather. I'm the latter.

Five inches of snow covered the ground when I arrived. At least six have fallen since. Odin wasn't thrilled when I asked him for a ride. He's even less thrilled now.

"You sure you want to do this, Alpha?" Odin asks.

"Did I not make myself clear the first time?" I ask.

The snarl to my voice returns his full concentration to the road. He's all but cowering now. It's not my intent. It's just me and how I feel.

As hard as it for someone like Odin to submit to me, it's easier away from his pack. He doesn't have to worry about looking weak in front of others, especially those he oversees.

Away from his pack, it's obvious, I scare. I'm not proud of it, just stating a fact.

Odin...you can say he was surprised to see me this soon. I imagine he never expected us to cross paths, again. I thought the same thing. But there I was, racing back to Somerville with those blasted pieces of broken wood clutched in my hands.

I tracked Odin back to his apartment and showed up unannounced with the aroma of dark magic spilling from me. He was less than thrilled when I dropped the broken pieces that housed the spell at his feet. The wolves surrounding him eased away from it, recognizing the evil it had contained. To Odin's credit, he glared at it, but held his ground.

"You told me nothing happens within a hundred-mile radius without you knowing about it," I reminded him. I leaned in to make it clear I wasn't asking. "Take me to whoever cast this."

When he shook his head slowly, I thought he was denying me. Then, a special kind of rage built inside him and it's like he wanted to help. "There's only one witch who could do that around here," he said. "And that bitch should have died long ago."

He grabbed his coat and keys and led me out, leaving Darra, another bear in charge.

"Alpha, we've heard things about you," Odin says, keeping his voice easy. "Around here, they speak about you like you 're some kinda chosen one. They say your strength is unlike any other *were*, and that you'll kill anything that crosses you."

I don't respond. My kind has always believed me greater than I am, like I'll someday rid the world of evil. No one can do that. But kill anything that crosses me? I won't deny that much.

"They also say you're good people," Odin adds.

"What?" I ask.

Something in my features make him laugh. "The *weres* you train, and those who stand by you, regard you like a god or something." You're hard on them, but your heart is as strong as your power."

Those who stand with me...could he mean my friends? Have they forgiven me? I shake my head. *No. Not after all the time's I've turned them away.*

"Alpha, from what I saw tonight, I believe what they say about you. But let me just say this, that bitch Griselda is crazy. She turned on and killed her own family, tortured, and hurt children. She has more power than any witch in the Northeast. You piss her off, you wind up dead."

"I don't plan to offend her," I clarify. "I just plan to tear her throat out."

Odin doesn't argue, not with the way my wrath thickens the small space between us.

He shifts uncomfortably as we pass an elementary school where only security lights cut through the gloom. The sign "Happy Winter Break" is barely visible through the mound of snow piled against it. I wouldn't call it happy, except it seems I'm all alone.

The whole area is like a winter wonderland. As we transition into a neighborhood, Christmas lights twinkle from frosted windows and ancient trees. These are older houses, nice and perched on lavish properties. Those inside have planned for a nice Christmas. They'll have it, and so will Celia.

Odin rolls to a stop in front of a light. "For alls our sake, I hope you take Griselda out, Alpha. If you don't, one day, the task will fall on me."

In his voice, I'm certain he means it. Still, I don't count on giving him the chance.

A snowplow bowls through the road parallel to us, creating a path where there was nothing more than a drift before. I prefer the drift. It's natural, unlike what waits ahead.

The light marks the border between the cities. The nice old homes shrink away to the quiet, safe streets behind us. Ahead, rows of dilapidated buildings await, the windows boarded, and exhaust-stained snow piled along the curb.

"I talked to the wolf in charge of the Upstate New York pack," Odin says, luring me from the level of poverty ahead. "He's coming with a few of his own after New Year's. Says he wants to talk to me and take a look at what I'm doing and what all I've done." He pauses. "He said if everything checks out, he'll help us, give us money to get started, and even set up our own Den in time. He's a *pure*, like you."

I smirk. I can't help it. "You say it like it's a bad thing."

"For some of us, it is a bad thing," he says. "*Was* a bad thing at least."

Pures are few and far between. Although we're considered royalty and held in high esteem, it's just a title as far as I'm concerned. Some of our kind see us as elitist. They're unaware as pures, we're dutybound to help *weres* like those in Odin's pack. At least, in theory we are.

For all I've talked up ridding the world of evil these past few years, the only *were* I've helped is myself.

"He listened to what I had to say," Odin continues. "He didn't like some things I did and told me I needed to make changes. But he listened, ya know? No one like him has listened to me in a long time."

I bow my head, mostly ashamed. I wouldn't have listened to Odin, either. I was too trapped in my own problems, until Celia.

"I owe you Alpha, you and your female."

I keep my gaze ahead. "You owe me nothing," I say. "Just get me to the Griselda. I'll take care of the rest. But, if something happens to me, I need you to swear you'll protect her."

There's no hesitation. "I'll swear it," he replies. "Maybe we can absorb her into the pack or somethin'.

"Celia doesn't belong in a pack." I scoff. "I don't know if her and her family belong anywhere. They're different and..." And what? I'm not sure how she'll manage without me? "Just make sure you watch out for her, without her knowing you're watching out for her." I almost smile. Almost. "She won't like that."

"No, she won't, will she?" he says, laughing.

The urban setting, I remember too well, fades away morphing from beatdown streets to better kept multi-family homes. Odin cuts a right down Woodland Avenue. Old Victorians in need of repair pop into view before transitioning into smaller, older homes. I should take it all in, I suppose. This is where my Celia grew up. All it does is remind me of what happened here and fires me up to get where I need to be.

We pass Maxon Middle School, where blue-collared residences make up the street. In the next block, the area abruptly changes. I straighten, no longer certain I can trust Odin.

Cookie-cutter old is replaced with long-standing, distinguished Tudors and sprawling mansions.

"I thought you said Griselda lived in Plainfield," I say.

"Easy, Alpha," Odin tells me. "This here is Plainfield, close to its neighbor South Plainfield, but still Plainfield. A long time ago, this was the place to be before it all turned to shit. The gay community is now taking over, bringing back the history of this place. They still have a long way to go, but this part here has benefitted." He motions to the right. "You hit Park Avenue, where the old hospital used to be, and you'll find what's left of 'Doctor's Row.' All dem doctors, lawyers, and such, had their businesses all up in there. In time, maybe the rich folk will do right by this city. Or they may forget about it all over again."

He cuts the lights and rolls to a stop behind a three-story Victorian. He points. "Griselda lives in the brown and white Tudor on the left, just past this house. A high metal gate surrounds the property. Front yard is smaller, backyard goes back almost an acre." He grins, not that there's much humor behind it. "You didn't expect Griselda to live like we've been livin', did ya? In small-assed apartments we barely make rent on?"

I shake my head. "No. But I didn't expect this." Snow slides down the roof when I open the door. I pull off my shirt and toss it into the cabin. For the first time tonight, it was actually dry. My jeans are still damp. They'll be harder to tear through, so I lose them along with everything else.

Odin's expression remains firm. "You don't need to do this by yourself, Alpha. My pack and I've got you."

"No," I order. "You have enough to explain to the alpha without adding a coven of dead witches to your resume."

He leans back into his seat, his right hand still at the wheel. "You gonna kill all of them?" he asks.

"Probably. If they aid Griselda, they're just as guilty." I shrug. "If they run, I may spare them, or I may not."

"Depends on your wolf?" Odin asks. "How mad he get?"

I understand his question. Beasts are harder to control when their counterparts are just as angry. Regardless, I'm the one in charge. "The spell alone gives me cause to kill her and anyone who kept her in power."

"And because she hurt your woman?" Odin asks.

That goes without saying.

Odin let's out a long whistle when more of my fury pokes through. "I get it, Alpha. Just you remember, Griselda didn't become who she is by being weak."

I meet his gaze then. "Neither did I."

Chapter Fourteen

I cross the street on four paws. Odin doesn't take off like I instructed him, too. The hunt is on. His beast wants in on it, too.

That's on him. I can't think about it. My wolf has waited for his chance to appear. I won't deny him any further.

I cut through the neighboring yard, the gray and white of my fur blending in with the night and snow. There are no Christmas lights illuminating Griselda's estate and those on either side of it. When you worship the wrong side, it eventually extends to areas surrounding it, invading like an infection until all hope vanishes.

As I reach the rear of the property, there's no slowing me down. I leap over the fence and stalk my first victim. He's tall, catching a smoke beside an old oak. He seems bored. Why wouldn't he be? Nothing sane would invade Griselda's home.

Damn shame for him, my wolf is bordering on psycho.

I hunch low on the ground, my paws sinking into the snow with barely a whisper of sound.

He's not human. He senses me, pushing away from the tree to look behind him. His eyes widen when he spots me. It's already too late. My jaws sink through his neck, slicing through tendons and muscles like a cleaver through sunbaked cheese.

The taste of vampire barely tickles my gums before I realize what he is.

Man, I *hate* vamps. For him to side with a witch either means he's a stray Griselda scooped up, or payment from a master. If it's the latter, he was exchanged for a debt or a deal. I don't care. This time, vamps aren't my problem.

I force my wolf to kill him quick. He only does it knowing more prey awaits. The vamp vanishes in a cloud of ash. The few bits of blood that remain on my fangs dry the same way. I step over his cigarette as the last bit of smoke dwindles in the air, eager to keep going and find my next victim.

The house sits on a hilltop. I ease my way down the incline, keeping low and using the landscape for coverage. Lights illuminate the rear of the house and laughter drifts over the melody of a well-played harp.

Griselda is celebrating the winter solstice while my love pushes aside her terror to comfort those she loves. To add to the insult, there's no indication she's aware the spell is broken. How arrogant do you have to be to think your spells are too ominous to destroy?

My growls vibrate across the small tree line, disappearing into the wind that picks up and shakes clumps of snow loose from the overhanging branches.

"Lawrence?" My next prey calls out.

His steps are loud as his hiking boots press into the snow. "Your turn inside." He tries to hide the nervousness in his voice. I'm sure the shit he's seen is unlike anything he signed up for.

The fear he emanates, and the silver crucifix laid over his black jacket, alert me he's human, and stupid to the way things work around here. Crosses and holy pendants are mere accessories to vampires. There's no heaven or hell to strive for or fear. You give up aging and gain beauty. That's the deal, in exchange for your soul. If you're killed, you simply stop being more than a memory to those selfless enough to recall your name.

This guy is former military or cop. His stance and how he carries himself gives him away. There's nothing real to protect him except for the gold bullets I scent lodged within his gun.

They'll do him no good. Griselda should have warned him *weres* are a lot faster to move than he is to draw.

His hand barely lifts in the direction of the holster at his hip when I shoot out and tackle him.

The crunch of his head hitting the brick walkway grants me some satisfaction but not enough. Not when I see what awaits inside.

From the windows of a large dining room, I see them. Girls as young as Emme and a little older than Celia stand naked in a circle. Shock riddles the features of those too afraid to cry. They clutch each other, their gazes giving away their dread.

A woman with hair as white as her skin carries a silver platter of appetizers. Her face expressionless as she stops at each table, offering caviar-covered shrimp and bruschetta to the witches in attendance.

Griselda sits on a throne at the head table, a crown of jewels perched upon her head. Most witches use precious stones to enhance and support the magic they're born with. Usually, they fasten them to a talisman around their necks or to a staff. Griselda, queen bitch that she is, needed more than one stone and a crown to support each.

Long dark hair brushes her shoulders as she sways drunk from her obscene power, while her brown skin illuminates her cold amber eyes. She's slender. She would be a beautiful woman if hatred didn't swim along her irises like sharks.

Her arrogance works to my advantage. She doesn't suspect or fear an attack. She's too immersed in the magic she's cultivated. Those stones at her crown weren't ones she earned by dedicating herself to her craft. She took them from witches she murdered.

Man, the evil she created coats my tongue with bitterness even from here. It's going to take perseverance not to gag when I rip her throat out.

Doesn't matter. I'll take my chances.

I ease my way down. They're expecting Lawrence. I need to move fast. I stick to the shadows, extending my senses as I watch the scene unfold.

A vampire yanks a young woman with dark skin toward him, breaking the spell holding the women in. He bites down on her jugular and makes a show of feeding from her. When he finishes, he drops her on the floor and walks away as if she's nothing.

The woman, clutches her neck, using her legs to return to the circle. She wants to cry yet is either too scared or too angry to permit those tears to fall. Good for her. She'll recover. I just need to get her out.

It's what I think when another vampire appears. The women scream as the she-vamp pulls out the same bleeding woman.

What the hell?

Vampires only need a pint of blood every few days. With the number of vamps waiting their turn, it doesn't appear Griselda permits them regular feeds. The woman's throat is mangled. Griselda won't even allow her vamps to seal the wounds with a few flicks of their tongue. The woman must have defied Griselda, and Griselda is making her pay.

Two other witches with dark hair sit on either side of Griselda. Their aroma of darkness that mimics Griselda's power tag them as her daughters. The witches gathered appear disgusted by the display of power, and some of their subordinates are as frightened as the young women in the circle. These clans are not here by choice. Griselda is flexing her muscles, and they're obliged to watch.

The witch on Griselda's right, a younger prettier version of Griselda, passes her a dagger with an ivory hilt. Griselda smiles and motions toward the circle with a tilt of her chin. The young witch smiles, the dark purple stone clasped to her amulet casting light across the room as she calls a young girl with red hair forth.

She's a blood sacrifice. So are the rest.

The young witch straightens, her voice a venomous purr she doesn't bother hiding. "Mami, do you feel it?" she asks. "Our master is most pleased. Allow these to quench his thirst." She leans in, her wicked glee escalating. "If they don't suffice, the other *putas* beneath you will."

The realization is as mind-blowing as my arrival.

This isn't a regular solstice. Griselda is celebrating a cursed noël.

The deity Griselda worships expects payment for making Griselda unstoppable. Thousands of blood sacrifices were made along the years for this moment to arrive. These girls, the witches, they're part of the fee. Celia and her family are the remaining balance.

My Celia.

The young redhead quivers, her gaze blank as she stumbles forward. My tail twitches, but it's the next vampire who pulls the leeched woman from the circle that calls me to action.

Glass rakes across my fur as I soar through the window, the scent of my power and magic inciting the starving vampires to attack.

Screaming and urges to run vibrate along the walls as I clamp down on a female vampire's throat. I shake her hard, snapping her neck to make her easier to kill.

Blood spouts as I slice through her carotid artery, sending the vampires into a frenzy.

I toss her to the side. Two vampires scramble after her, the promise of nourishment too much to ignore. They latch onto the female vamp and suck her dry, giving me time to go after the others.

Ash coats my back as I puncture the heart of the next vampire. He's weak and dies easily, so does the next. That's what Griselda gets for allowing her vampires to teeter so close to bloodlust.

The witch to Griselda's left calls out, her voice urgent through the escalating screams of fleeing witches. "Mami, *it's him*," she says. "The wolf who haunts your dreams."

I growl low and deep. *No. I'm the wolf from your* fucking *nightmares.*

I expect a good fight. I'm outnumbered. But the other witch clans have seen enough.

Multi-colored lights from firing amulets pelt my fur as witches disappear in a crash of thunder or race to the exits with their brethren close to their heels.

Not all leave. A spell cast from a lingering warlock singes my fur when he launches it. I feel it approach, sparing my body from the brunt of it, but not the vampire I use as a shield.

The vamp collapses on the marble floor. He chokes on his screams when his limbs morph into vipers that shred him to pieces.

My wolf pushes out the small part of the spell that struck. The warlock, dumbstruck with terror that I survived, makes a mad dash to the foyer. He doesn't make it out of the dining room when I dive on top of him.

He drops his staff. I *change* to human and slam my heel into his back and crack his spine. I then grasp the staff and use it to stake the two vampires who remain.

Like the other vamps, they were young and weak. Still dangerous to humans, but nothing to an angry *were* like me.

The green-colored light permeating from the warlock's amulet fades as its master takes his last breath.

I stalk toward the young women, breaking the salt circle encasing them. The spell breaks with a sharp kick to my shins. I don't react. My attention is on Griselda as the shrieking and sobbing women run past me.

Griselda greets me with a smile. I greet her with a snarl.

At her nod, Griselda's youngest daughter charges. Her magic blurs her form and adds speed I'm ill-prepared for. I drop into a crouch and *change* as we crash through the wall.

The impact caves my sternum inward. I shove away the pain and the magic. She's young. Her curse was meant for a man, leaving my wolf plenty alive.

I *change* again, walking toward the young witch. She spits out several swears and gathers her magic. I swerve out of the way of the first strike and punch through the wall when I sense another attack. A warlock was calling upon his power. He never got a chance to cast his hex. I pull him through the wall by his throat and toss him at the witch. The entire ordeal takes only seconds. Enough time for me to react and for her to execute another spell.

The warlock is reduced to maggots that rain down on the young witch. She may enjoy turning her victims to maggots. But she doesn't like those maggots falling on her. I lift her over my head before she can recover and throw her against the metal railing of a long, majestic staircase.

A piece of railing breaks off from the force and punctures through her stomach. She's strong enough to shield her body, so the injury doesn't kill her. She's just not strong enough to break free or heal. She shrieks, her feet kicking as I step back into the dining room.

The remaining daughter charges me, throwing wine-colored fire that reeks of brimstone. I leap up and grasp the edges of a large chandelier and swing, bringing down the ceiling all over her. I land in a crouch and stalk toward the quivering mound of debris.

She stands in an explosion of flame, this time striking me head on. Like Griselda, this witch has racked up her share of kills. I won't be one of them.

I *change* and jump back into the foyer, landing in a roll against a wool rug. I spin back and forth, extinguishing the flames eating away at my fur before I high-tail it back to the dining room.

Griselda's daughter casts another curse. The fire she targets me with this time is wider and more difficult to avoid. I swerve and leap, narrowly side-stepping each shot. The room pays the price, as well as Griselda's belongings.

The flames eating away at the walls spikes the temperature in the room and invigorates the logs burning in the fireplace. A painting ignites, followed by several old photos, and some art pieces that must be worth a fortune.

The young witch, frustrated with the damage she's inflicting onto everything except her intended target, gives up on torching me. With a frustrated yell, she launches tables and chairs in my direction, including Griselda's abandoned throne.

I avoid the table and most of the chairs, roaring when a table leg knocks me in the shoulder and takes me down. I *change* into human again and lift the staff belonging to the dead warlock.

The young witch leaps with freakish height, manifesting fire around her willowy frame to protect her. Like a batter gunning for the winning run, I smash the staff across her face.

Bone shatters in a loud crack as she goes flying. She lands near the window amidst all the debris.

She doesn't move. She doesn't do much of anything. I toss the staff and resume my wolf form.

Flames chew through the walls, the holes in the ceiling allowing me to see that the fire has already reached the second floor. I have time before the house starts breaking apart. Just enough to find Griselda.

I search, and find her in a solarium, seemingly gliding as she examines the plants.

Cold, black and white checkered tile greets my paws. I welcome how it soothes the battered skin my wolf is only beginning to heal.

"I didn't expect to see you this soon," Griselda tells me. She breaks off a white rose from its bush and inhales deep. "Did the little bitch who holds your heart call you to her?" She crushes the rose between her fingertips as she turns to face me, the petals spilling along the floor. She laughs. "I suppose it doesn't matter, does it, young alpha?"

Shrieks of terror and pain erupt from outside. The noise fades abruptly, muffled by the decibels of sound clanging in my ears. Something sinister has just struck me across the face. I gag on the bitter taste, barely cognizant of the curse Griselda cast against me.

I fall down the stairs of my house, each step my back strikes threatening to snap my spine.

My body curls inward when I land. I don't remember ever feeling this much pain. Whimpers, small and pathetic, push my lip in and out. I look up, my vision blurring.

Someone with big, heavy feet walks down as my sight begins to clear. I see boots and the faded jeans of someone with very long legs. He's coming. He's not done hurting me yet.

Small hands that are part of my small body, slide along the slick wooden floors. I try to lift myself up, but I'm too fragile.

I have to get up. I made him mad and he's going to kill me.

"Aric!"

Celia calls to me, her voice morphing into my mother's as Mom kneels beside me. She pushes my hair from my face, disappointment wrinkling her features.

"You're weak," Mom tells me. "Too pathetic to be our son."

I lift my chin to see my dad. He swings his foot and kicks me in the face.

My nose shatters and the left side of my face droops awkwardly. I try to move my mouth. All I feel is agony.

A stab to my chest follows, causing my lung to collapse.

"You're no son of mine," Dad yells. "I should have killed you when you were inside of her."

My mother walks toward me, rubbing her belly and cooing to the baby inside of her. "This one will be better," she promises.

"Aric," Celia calls again. "*Aric*!"

Another stab, this one just missing my heart. Mom sits beside me. Her voice frustrated. "Aric," she says.

"*Aric*!" Celia roars.

"It's her," someone hollers.

Mom shakes her head, yelling over her shoulder. "Why can't she just die!"

She turns back to me. "You didn't listen to your father. Now, he'll make you pay."

My father marches toward me, ready to cast his final blow. My mother lifts the knife.

I push up and leap, breaking through the spell I'm encased in and lunge toward Griselda.

The dagger she used to stab me spins when it hits the floor. The spinning sound slows as I paint the walls with her blood.

I lied to Odin. I don't rip out her throat as much as I shred it, and her, into pieces. It doesn't take me long. I'm more than motivated to do it.

After I finish, I step over her body and pad toward the front door.

No one bothered to close it. No witch. No human. They were too busy trying to live.

It seems the same goes for Griselda's daughters. They're gone as well.

Fine. Their reputations were linked to their mother. She's gone and won't be coming back. Without her, it's only a matter of time before they meet the same fate.

Had they been stronger. Had more witches stayed to fight. Had the vamps not been so weak. Yeah, I might not have made it.

I discover the reason why I survived perched on the front porch.

A golden tigress sits at the top of the stairs, her tail twitching back and forth as she admires the carnage below. Enough blood was shed to color the front yard red.

Griselda's backup had apparently arrived. All human. All armed with guns. It's only the aroma of fresh falling snow that muffles enough cursed gold bullets to take on a pack.

Her small army was expecting a wolf. A big cat with an attitude is all they found.

Celia was more than enough, and she still is.

Odin and his *weres* wait along the driveway, giving Celia, and I suppose me, ample space. The bear, the one he left in charge, hands him a folded blanket. He takes it, walking slowly toward where we wait on the wide stone steps.

It's almost dawn. The trickles of light that snow allows through, illuminates the golden tigress. Her fur is stained with mud and human life. She shudders, *changing* to leave her human counterpart trembling in the cold.

I *change*, taking the blanket Odin offers and wrapping it around me and Celia.

"We'll take care of the mess, Alpha," he says. He looks around, stating the obvious. "Looks to me like Griselda won't be hurting your woman again."

Celia's voice shakes from the cold and much more than I can spare her from. "I made the pack bring me," she says. She tries to motion to the dead men. "They-they were going to kill you. I-I-I couldn't let them."

I gather Celia to me, embracing her with my warmth and wishing more than anything my love alone could ease her pain.

Chapter Fifteen

The crunch of snow along the driveway and the *beep, beep,* from the car's horn announce the girls' departure. Ana Lisa is tucked in the back, covered with blankets she insisted she didn't need and doted on by Emme who can't seem to leave her side.

We wave, watching them disappear down the block. I thought I would have to carry Ana Lisa to the car. But with the nullits gone, she's regained enough strength to independently leave her bed. It's a huge step. I pray her tenacity will give her more time with those she loves.

Celia shuts the door and locks it tight. "Are you sure you don't want to go with them?" I'm asking out of courtesy, and not because I haven't looked forward to being alone with her.

Celia turns to face me, brushing a strand of her wavy hair away from her face. "Amalay, her other foster daughter, has a cat." She smiles, her bright eyes lighting up as she takes me in. "Let's just say I'm allergic to it."

I don't think she means it the way that it sounds. I don't argue. What I do is turn away.

There are things in life that are almost too beautiful to look at. Celia is one of them.

I step into the family room, taking in the stockings at the hearth, fuzzy and beaten down with time, and the small plastic tree we lugged down from the attic, whose lights add color and brightness to the small space.

The mess we made last night is gone. Mostly due to Taran's obsession with perfection and Emme's mad telekinetic skills.

Don't get me wrong, the house isn't perfect. Not by a long shot. The aroma of Ana Lisa's medication still drifts from her room and the air is heavy knowing her time is limited. Yet somehow, it's perfect enough, and ready for tomorrow.

When I'm gone, everything will return to the way it was. I accomplished my mission. The nullits are gone, the curse is broken, and Griselda is dead.

Good. I only wish it was enough.

I won't be here for the next big bad when it comes. Celia and her family will be on their own. Will she survive without me? I bow my head. I guess she'll have to.

I just don't know how I'll survive without her.

My legs ease me into a crouch. I lift the ornament Shayna made me from the floor. She used her power to manipulate a few quarters into a wolf, insisting I needed my very own ornament. More teddy bear than *were,* and too heavy for the wobbly branches, I pass my thumb over its face before placing it beside one of Celia's.

Shayna was kind to include me.

Emme cried upon our return.

Taran almost fried me when I carried Celia in naked.

She got over it, mostly. "If you knock up my sister, I'll burn your man parts to cinders."

I'm pretty sure she meant it. Given she also slapped a strip of condoms in my hand before stomping out the door.

Celia wraps her arms around my waist and presses a kiss between my shoulder blades.

"Not everyone gets a happy ending, do they?" she asks quietly.

"No," I agree almost silently. My parents are living proof.

"But we're different," I add. "We're going to make it."

"Promise?" she asks.

I squeeze my eyes shut, trying not to think about all the things that can go wrong and how evil itself seems to want these girls dead. "My love," I say. "We have to."

In the quiet that follows, I fixate on the television. Shayna found a channel that plays holiday music with a crackling fireplace for a background.

"You need ambiance," she insisted. "You know, in case you deflower my sister."

Emme ran away. Ana Lisa pretended not to hear; I think. She's a realist, and for what it's worth, I think she likes me.

Stevie Nick's version of *Silent Night* begins to play. The ache building in my throat makes it hard to swallow. Maybe it's Celia's warm presence against me, but I can't remember the song affecting me this much.

Celia skims her fingers back and forth, loosening the fabric of my T-shirt from the waistband of my jeans. "What am I supposed to do without you, wolf?" she asks.

I turn around and grip her hips. She's already crying. I'm not far behind.

Males aren't supposed to cry.

We keep our emotions bottled in tight.

Except no real male stands a chance against true love.

Celia, my God, she's all heart. And she's pounding mine to dust.

"I can't answer that," I reply, truthfully. I raise her chin, my voice raw. "Not when I don't know how I'll live without your smile." She blushes. I grin but it pains me. "Yeah, that, too."

Christmas is tomorrow.

She and her family are safe.

It's time for me to go.

I wish I could throw something or kill those nullits all over again. Damn, I'm so angry that I have to leave her vulnerable and alone.

Mimi won't permit my presence much longer. I'm waiting to evaporate into thin air or maybe go out in a fiery explosion. I can't tell with Mimi.

Just like I can't tell my Celia goodbye.

The condoms Taran gave me are practically burning a hole through my pocket. I guide Celia to the couch. I want to hold her. Hell, there's a lot I want to do to her. But I don't want to force or rush her. So, I release her, and place my forearms along my thighs.

My eyes sting and my throat is on fire with desperate words I wish I could say.

"Tell me something about you," I tell her.

"What?" she asks. She gives it some thought. Yeah, she heard me. "What do you want to know?"

I angle my chin to face her. "Anything."

She smiles, even as a tear drop falls from her chin to wet her jeans. "I want babies," she says.

"*What?*"

She laughs, her face heating. "Not now, wolf." Her humor fades, just enough to leave her small smile. "I lost my parents too soon and I found Ana Lisa too late." She sighs. "I want babies to call my own, to raise and never let them go."

"You want a family," I say slowly.

I'm not trying to make her cry. Yet another tear splashes against her jeans. "I want to give what I didn't receive, and love in a way I was denied." She pauses as if unsure of herself. "Is that wrong?"

I shake my head. "No. I want what was taken from me, too."

I force my breathing to slow. God, it's like every cell is screaming for air, threatening to suffocate me without her beside me. I can't leave her. I just fucking can't.

"What are you thinking?" she asks.

Again, I don't want to upset her except I don't want to lie either. "That I can't imagine a world where we don't end up together."

She clasps her hands over her eyes and chokes back a sob. I

gather her against me, wishing I could kick my own ass for hurting her. "If I'm really yours, find me, okay?" she says. "Whatever you do, don't let me live a life without you."

"I'll find you. I swear it." I mean what I say. But in a world of billions, how is that even possible? I'm supposed to be this bigshot now, right? I'm supposed to fill that role my kind always knew I would. If that's true, my responsibilities can take me anywhere. Where will the world take her?

And what will it do to her while I'm gone?

She looks up at me, her eyes shimmering with her tears. "Aric, no one makes me feel the way you do. But what if you find someone, before you find me?"

"*Never.*"

I cup her face and smash our lips together. The move is quick and fierce, more animalistic than anything my human half has ever performed. But it's the silkiness behind my touch and the uninhibited desire I feel that sends my pulse racing.

Her hands slide to hold my face as our kiss intensifies. My fingers drag down her back to find the edge off her long-sleeved shirt. I pull it off her in one move, her long hair fanning her shoulders in a soft cascade. My skin, so alive with her this close to me, heats further when I tear off my shirt and it hits the floor.

Celia rises, goosebumps spreading along her flat stomach as her hips sway back and forth and she shifts out of her jeans. I stand, gripping her waist and lifting her so her legs lock around me. She tightens her hold, moaning as I nibble her skin, and slide a finger down the rear of her thong.

I tug it, teasing her and teasing me. Just one hard pull. That's all it will take to rid her of it and take that final step. Will she deny me? I hope not. But any harm to her will crush me that much more.

A growl escapes my lips when she drags her nails down my back and rocks her pelvis against mine.

My voice is raspy, hardening like the rest of me. "Tell me how to make you feel good," I whisper.

"I..."

It's all she says. Maybe it's all she knows.

I don't know what I'm doing, either. I'm merely listening to her body to show me how to please her.

Her back arches as I trail soft and not so soft kisses down her throat. The heat simmering between us is more than I can take. I kick out of my boots and carelessly strip out of my socks and shirt. My jeans remain, so do my boxers. Those are hers to remove when and if she's ready.

I hope she's ready. I am.

I don't mean to rip her clothes off—never mind, yes, I do. My kisses sweep over the swell of her breasts. My teeth, they find the center of her bra. I pull hard. It's a playful move and more than enough.

The fabric tears and her breasts fall free. For a moment I merely breathe her in, taking these last few bits of time to worship her sensual form.

Her panties are now all she has left.

Yet it's too much for what I want to do to her.

I kiss her again before flicking my tongue over her breasts. My teeth graze each tip, tightening them further.

Celia's grunts, her eyes alternating between hers and her beast's. "You have experience," she rasps.

"No," I answer truthfully. "All I know is how bad I want you."

She fumbles to remove what remains of her bra. I lower her, sliding off her panties as I trace a path with my tongue past her belly. She shudders, reaching for me to balance, and nearly falling over when I bury my face between her thighs.

Celia whimpers, the sounds of our lovemaking become more pronounced as I taste her soft flesh. I hold her sides to keep her in place. She jolts, screaming when I find a good rhythm.

I lift my head, my heart hammering my ribcage with how much I need to be inside her. "Tell me to stop," I say, hoping she doesn't deny me.

I'll stop. I swear I will if she tells me.

But like me, she's ready.

She threads her fingers through my hair and shakes her head. "There's nothing I won't let you do to me."

She urges me to stand, guiding me to her bedroom as the Christmas tree lights paint her bare form. We're only just inside her room when her hand disappears in my jeans and...

One slow stroke follows another.

And another.

She quickens her motions, watching me clamp my jaw with the increasing force of her pulls. I reach for the condoms and toss them on the bed. I try to lead us there except she drops to her knees and takes me in her mouth.

My head spins, her touch, her aroma of water misting across roses, *everything* about her makes me lose it. I reach toward the bed to retrieve a condom. She stops me with another deep taste and slides one in place.

I lift her, kissing her as I place her on her bed.

Her back slides along the cool sheets.

Her thighs fall open.

She's ready.

So, I am.

Celia mews as I make my way in, each small thrust of my hips advancing me further inside her. I'm huge. No lie. And she's so small.

Each motion is barely there. I don't want to hurt her. As much as I'm ready for our bodies to join, I wait, each press forward cautious and cognizant of her needs.

Celia kisses me, opening herself further. "I love you," I tell her. "God, I love you so much."

When we finish, it doesn't seem real. We can't stop kissing or smiling or loving. I tossed two condoms we used in the garbage and retrieved my clothes and hers when I brought us some water.

She laughs when I nuzzle her neck. I think we'll go again when I stroke her face and my hand begins to fade.

We startle, our eyes widening. "No," she says.

My skin grows cold. Almost immediately, I feel her slipping away.

"Aric, no." She glances around, as if she can somehow use something to stop me. "Please. Don't leave me."

I pull her against me, cursing Mimi and everything taking me away from Celia.

I won't wake beside her.

Tomorrow, I won't see her, or the next day after that.

Her life will move forward without me.

But how the *fuck* will I move forward without her?

Although I speak within my thoughts, what feels like shards of glass rake against each syllable. *Will you remember me?*

No, Mimi replies, her harsh voice soft, just this once. *Nor will you recall anything about her.*

Why? Why do this to me—to her? I demand.

Aric Connor, for you to become the man you're meant to be, you must forget. And for her to become the tigress the world needs, she must forget the man you are, Mimi answers.

Celia curls against me, her tears soaking my chest. It takes all I have not to tear this house apart.

Have faith, young alpha, Mimi tells me. *You won't remember, but your wolf* always *will.*

What is that supposed to mean?

Mimi doesn't answer me, not in the way I want her to.

The window flies open, and a strong wind seeped with Mimi's magic flows through the room. Snowflakes flicker over us, spinning gently to melt against our skin.

Celia tries to blink away her tears, but they form faster and trickle into her words. "I can't tell you goodbye," she says. "Just know that I love you, okay? *Please*, don't forget that I love you."

Her sorrow worsens and her barely-there voice disappears in the escalating breeze. I clutch her to me as the current surrounding us intensifies.

It's time to go. No way in hell am I ready to leave. I tuck her closer, hanging onto this small moment of paradise where we became one.

"I love you," she tells me again. "I'll always love you."

It kills me to look at her. I do, anyway. Memorizing her small delicate features, those green eyes that dig like arrows launched from her soul, that beautiful face I'd destroy a thousand armies for, and that heart mine will never rightfully beat without.

I wept when we buried the remains of my father. Allowing only three tears to fall, one for anger, the other for grief, the last one for love.

And I weep now, the three tears that glide down my cheeks *all for love*.

I bite out the words of yet another agonizing goodbye. "It's time," I say.

Whether it's Mimi's magic pulling me away or perhaps the little mercy she has to give, Celia's head drops against my shoulder, and she fades into a deep sleep.

I don't remember what my life was like without her. I don't remember feeling much of anything, from the rocks my bare feet slapped against back home, or the feel of that first cold rain that comes with fall.

I only remember Celia, her scent, her touch, her warmth.

I fight the pull of Mimi's magic, my wolf howling in agony.

Everything hurts.

Everything in me tells me this is wrong.

Her skin feels cold without me.

Who will keep her warm?

Who will keep her safe?

Who will keep her heart?

I want to be that male she needs, the one the world needs to stand beside her when the time comes. I want to demonstrate the integrity, intelligence, and courage my father always expected. It's only then will I come close to deserving her love.

Damn. There's so much pain. For me, and my wolf.

I howl as I'm torn away from her, the torment of our separation more than I can bear. As she fades from sight, the spirit of my wolf jets away from me and into her.

I think he's gone. But it was just a part of him.

Just enough of me to give to her.

Chapter Sixteen

Mimi is a fucking nutcase.

It's my only thought as I roll to my knees and rub the mini-drumline marching across my head.

My eyelids fly open when I see her on her back, her little feet twitching and her toes smoking. I rush forward and tilt her up.

She coughs the smoky remains of her spell into my face and grins at me with the four teeth she has left. She scrutinizes me closely. "That should do it," she says with a nod.

I glance around the burnt surroundings that used to be my backyard. The woodpile is glowing with embers and the pump is nothing more than a warped piece of metal. The roof of Dad's old shed caves in and the whole thing falls on its side.

What's left of the well-cover crackles and disintegrates, falling with a splash. The only reason I don't snap Mimi's neck is that the house is untouched.

"You set everything on fire!" I growl.

Mimi frowns at me and gives me the onceover. Her frown relaxes and her beady eyes twinkle with enough naughty to shame a skin magazine. "That's not all I did for you. Is it, young alpha?"

"Huh?"

Her tiny fist punches me affectionately in the shoulder. "You're welcome," she replies.

Mimi shuffles to her still smoking toes and bats at her dirt-crusted backside. "Your mama must be hungry." She hobbles in the direction of what might be a shoe, taking in her handywork with more pride than humiliation. "I suggest take out."

I open my mouth to growl. Before I can, the crazy old hag vanishes.

I kick away the remains of an ax and head to the house to check on Mom. Mimi is out of control, unreasonable, and way too sure of herself.

My foot hovers over the next step as shame takes a hold of me. "Hey, kettle, you're just as bad as pot," I mutter.

I push forward and into the kitchen. I find several cans of stew in the pantry. It's from that stockpile Mom always kept for those times when the weather was too bad too hunt. She never wanted me or Dad to go hungry.

Dad. Yeah, he always watched out for us, too.

The stew isn't much, but it's enough. I heat it quickly and run up to Mom. She's right where I left her, staring at the picture of dad holding me as baby. He always gave us everything. She did the same.

There was just one thing they couldn't give each other.

The one thing I know I can.

"Mom, you can't keep doing this to yourself. You have to get better." I place the steaming bowl of stew on the nightstand and sit on the bed beside her.

"I don't know if I can, my darling," she says, her eyes never leaving the photo.

I help her to a sitting position and promise her something I likely have no business promising. "You have to, Mom." My words spill out before I can stop them. "I'm going to have babies one day, lots of them."

She stills, life shimmering through her eyes in a way I haven't seen in long time.

"Aric, don't say things like that," she says quietly. I think she's serious, yet there's that spark, that glimmer of hope.

"Unless I mean it?" I finish for her.

I blow out a breath. She's giving me an out. I don't bother taking it.

"I'm going to give you grandchildren one day, Mom. I swear I will." I swallow hard. "They're going to need you. Do you hear me? They're going to need all of us to survive."

TOUCH OF EVIL

A Weird Girls Novel

CECY ROBSON

Chapter One
Emme

There's a naked werewolf standing in front of me.

Let me kindly explain.

There's *a naked werewolf*—a man who can *change* into a wolf —standing naked, in human form, in front of me.

They do that a lot, *change* from beast to full naked glory. Typically, it's pre and post bloody battle for the sake of the world and to protect its unsuspecting human populace. However awkward, I'm used to it.

"Like what you see?" he asks.

Make that sort of used to it.

He flexes and gives a little thrust to show off what he thinks are some delectable goods and *oh, my*...he has three testicles.

I slap my hands over my eyes. I take it back. I take it all back. I'm not used to all *this*.

"Emme," Ted asks. "Did you just gag?"

I'm not a rude person.

I'm not a liar.

"Yes?" is my response.

Ted is a lot bigger than me. He's also stronger and can snap my spine without *changing* to his beast counterpart. I keep my hands over my eyes. As a nurse by trade, and a supernatural fighter by sheer terrible luck, I have seen things. Ugly, frightening, and unexceptionally evil things. And I've encountered creatures so menacing mere thoughts reduce me to trembles.

I draw the line at extra testicles.

The sound of slapping and bouncing skin causes me to shrink inward. Ted seems to be putting on quite the show. Honestly, it sounds like a one-man juggling act involving best-left-covered body parts.

I'm tired of dating Teds.

And humans, they wouldn't survive me or the world my sisters and I were thrown into.

No, in order to be with me you must have something special.

And I'm not referring to what Ted is currently playing with.

My hands slip away from my face when I sense his approach.

"In my world, I'm revered for my virility," he says to my back.

"Mm-hmm," I reply. I pity the packmate forced to run behind him.

Ted is either referring to his obscenely large member *weres* are known for ("They're built for attracting females," my perky sister once explained) or the extra semen sack dangling halfway down his thigh. Neither impress me and neither does Ted.

I carefully step over the second of two discarded pizza boxes and make my way toward the exit.

My steps slow as I reach the door.

I turn to my left, then to my right. Something else is here.

Dread and resentment drag their long spindly fingers across my skin and hate coats my tongue.

I'm scared and on guard, and it's not because of Ted.

My gaze skips around the apartment, past the galley kitchen and to the boarded window covered with a *Scarface* poster. I don't see anyone or anything else. What I sense though is wrong and it shouldn't be here.

I keep my voice quiet, not wanting whatever is here to hear me. "Do you feel that?" I ask.

"Yeah, baby," he says. "It feels good. How about you feel it, too?"

Forget it. Ted is on his own.

I grip the greasy knob, trying not to give too much thought as to why it's greasy, and more than anxious to leave Ted and his new roommate behind.

Ted slams his hand on the door above my head. It's a show of strength, reminding me that he's the one with the muscles and no matter how hard I pull, this door won't open unless he allows it.

Hot and heavy breath skitters along my neck, fluttering the strands of loose blonde hair that escaped my bun. He's aroused, like a wolf who's just caught his prey.

Except I'm not prey, no matter how much I resemble the part.

"I thought you were different, Emme," he whispers, this tenor pitch dropping low.

My hand slips away from the knob. "I thought you were different, too," I say.

There were no penis pics from Ted. No midnight booty calls while drunk on witch's brew. No inappropriate texts that made me blush or had me Googling terms like "pony play."

I did think Ted was different. Yet here I am, in a dirty apartment and in the company of another naked loser and... something else.

That sense of hate returns, surging along with a foreboding air of vengeance. Whatever is here is out for blood.

Ted skims his knuckles down my spine, adding another layer of "ew" with each pass. But it's that feeling that we're not alone that amplifies my need to escape.

I reach for the knob, again. It's useless, Ted keeps his position and the door firmly in place.

"You're making this a lot harder than it needs to be," I tell him. My eyes fix on the chipped gray paint covering the wood. Ted is under the impression he has me where he wants me. He fails to see I'm the one in control.

"You're the so-called 'sweet' one," Ted begins. "The innocent one of the Weird girls."

The insult draws my attention back to him. "Our last name is Wird," I correct. "And we're not a fan of that nickname."

Ted continues as if I never spoke. "I know better. Every hetero with a dick does. You fucked that vampire and fucked him good, no?"

His Creole accent was cute at first. Nothing of that cuteness remains. Heat builds along my cheeks, erasing the chills that the dark presence stirred.

My teeth clench hard. "You don't know what you're talking about."

"I also hear you're sad and lonely, desperate since your boyfriend was killed. You remember him, don't you? The same *were* who preferred a disfigured freak over you—"

I whip around, no longer feeling polite. "Don't you dare speak of Liam and his mate that way, and don't presume to know me."

"Relax, sugar tits. They can't hear me. They're dead, remember?"

I slap him across the face. It hurts. *Oh, it hurts.* I avoid shaking out the burn in my hand. The strike worked against me. He barely felt it. But he knows I felt his words.

Humiliation crawls across my face. Being *were,* he can sniff my pain and embarrassment. He laughs, bent on casting another blow. "Your brother-in-law is the Alpha Aric Connor, right chérie?"

The throbbing pain stiffening my fingers tightens my response. "Yes."

Aric is a revered pureblood and the strongest of his kind. His reputation alone cautions supernaturals against offending me. Ted, being new to Tahoe and naïve to Aric's power, doesn't understand he's about to cross a very dangerous line.

He bends to meet my face, his lascivious grin cutting lines into his narrow face.

"Just because you're related to the alpha by marriage doesn't make you anything special. If you want the truth, it's your sister Taran I wanted. She's as hot as the fire she casts with her magic. If she wasn't mated to the second in command, I would have fucked her harder than you did that vamp." He pushes off the door. "Now, run away, little girl. Keep living your lonely and pathetic life. Maybe next time, you'll appreciate the piddly scraps thrown your way."

Angry tears threaten to fall and sizzle across my burning face. His tirade struck almost every insecurity I possess.

Some beings make an art of out of inflicting pain. Ted should run a master class.

I square my shoulders. "It's one thing to not take rejection well," I say. "It's another to be cruel to spare your ego."

Ted shrugs. "Not cruel, chérie. *Honest.*" He straightens to his full height to look further down his long nose at me. "You're lucky," he says. "I don't usually waste my time with weaklings like you."

I blink back the tears I'm tired of shedding. "No, *you're lucky* I don't throw you out the window."

This really makes him laugh.

He stops laughing when I do, in fact, throw him out the window.

My *force*, the cool name my bubbly sister nicknamed my telekinetic power, funnels from my core and propels Ted and his might-mighty ego across the room. What remains of the boarded window explodes into shards of glass and splintering wood.

Ted lands with a thud, and plenty of swearing, three stories below with leftover window bits raining down on him.

I turn the knob and step into the open stairwell of Ted's apartment building, pausing when a warning pokes at me and reminds me I'm not alone.

The door shuts behind me with a creak. I look down the hall. To my right, only quiet awaits, the only signs of life from the reflection of a T.V. against a window. My way out is a different story.

A *were*, bear I believe, rests his back against a wall, speaking to what might be a cougar. I'm not like my sister Celia, whose inner tigress can scent a predator, or like Taran, who can distinguish supernaturals by the magic that surrounds them. I'm not even like Shayna. Since her mate's werewolf essence began residing inside her, she's learned to differentiate *weres* by instinct.

I do well enough, reaching out with my gift to discern the inner beasts lurking within them. The density of their musculature and the way they move and command their stances are very telling. Each characteristic mimics their animal counterparts. I've met many *weres* across the globe and have studied their traits closely. I'm certain I pegged them correctly. The others who appear, though, don't give me the time I need to distinguish them, and their collective power caution that now is not the time.

Weres ease out from their homes, joining those lingering along the stairwell. Some are male, most are female. They watch me closely, trying to pin what and who I am.

My sisters and I are different from any race of human or supernatural on earth. According to our wolves, we give off unique magical aromas that place humans and preternaturals on guard. While I understand, I don't enjoy the attention.

I adjust my purse against my side and walk forward with my head high, feigning confidence I wish came naturally instead of merely skimming the surface of my ivory skin. The purse was a new purchase to go with my blouse and skirt, efforts to look nice for someone I believed was decent.

Ted fooled me. We had dinner just a few blocks away, our conversation was pleasant and polite. There was no flirting and absolutely no sparks. I was sure we'd call it an early night so, his suggestion caught me by surprise. "Will you join me for a drive along the lake, chérie?" he asked. "It's the perfect night to take in the moon and sky."

I agreed and didn't give much thought when he told me we had to return to his apartment to fetch his keys.

There were no keys. No drive. No sky. Only nakedness and more sex organs than anyone should ever need.

"Hey, baby." The cougar steps into my path, the silky way he moves mesmerizing. This isn't someone who sleeps alone much.

"Now that your done with that fool Ted, let a real man show you a good time."

I start to tell him no, when the bear interrupts. He mashes out the cigarette on the sole of his ratty sneakers and pulls the cougar back by the arm. "Don't go there," he tells the cougar. "That there is Aric Connor's fam."

I don't see well in the dark. Not like Celia and the wolves do. But I do notice the cougar blanche.

He edges away with his hands up. "Sorry, uh, ma'am, I mean, miss. I didn't mean any disrespect."

"It's all right," I say. My chin trails down as I walk past them, only to snap up when that dark presence returns.

The *weres* growl in that way they do before something meets a gruesome and vomit-inducing death. I can't see their faces with their backs to me, but I recognize they're seconds from charging. The muscles lining their broad shoulders clench and their knees bend. They'll pounce and maul whatever is out here and anything that gets in their way.

A few feet down where the T.V. casts light against the window, another *were* throws open his door and steps out. I can't tell what he is, not from this distance. He's small, closer to my five-foot frame than the behemoths directly in front of me. A honey badger maybe?

"Did ya hear that?" he asks. His growl is lighter and more like a whine but just as fierce.

"Yeah, we did," the bear replies. He takes a strong whiff. "Fuck if it don't smell like shit."

I didn't hear what they did or catch the smell that alerted them. I adjust my hold on the purse straps and inch forward. The cougar's arm shoots out, warning me to stay put. "Get going, little one, before you get hurt. We'll handle this mess."

"I-I can help," I stammer. My voice reflects my raw mood. The experience with Ted eviscerated my heartstrings, and this thing, whatever it is, hasn't helped me settle. So instead of adding backbone to my words, my shaky voice validates the cougar's perceptions that I'm weak.

"Go, little one," the bear insists. "We don't want trouble from the alpha if you bleed."

"I can heal myself," I start to explain.

If they hear me, they don't show it. As a pack, they move as one, picking up their pace when that presence takes off in a sprint. The *weres* who remain perk up, eager to back their brethren. Several swing down from the stairwell overhead and jet after the cougar and bear, while more above race forward, their swift and collective steps barely perceptible.

The *weres* are quick to join the hunt.

And so am I.

Photo by Kate Gledhill of
Kate Gledhill Photography

Cecy Robson is an international and award-winning author who is published with Penguin, Random House, and Entangled Publishing.

As a registered nurse of twenty-one years, Cecy spends her free time creating magical worlds, heart-stopping romance, and young adult adventure. Her novels have been translated into multiple languages and are featured in CHAPTERS Interactive Story app., as well as HOOKED where Cecy writes as Rosalina San Tiago.

Cecy is honored to have received two RITA® nominations, the Maggie Award, and the Award of Excellence. She was also a finalist for the National Reader's Choice Award and the National Excellence in Story Telling. You can find Cecy laughing, crying, and cheering on her characters as she pens her next story.

Connect with Cecy online:

www.cecyrobson.com
Facebook.com/Cecy.Robson.Author
instagram.com/cecyrobsonauthor
twitter.com/cecyrobson
www.goodreads.com/CecyRobsonAuthor
tiktok.com/@cecyrobson

For exclusive information and more, join my Newsletter!
https://cecyrobson.com/newsletter.html